DETROIT PUBLIC LIBRARY

3 5674 05155063 1

CONELY BRANCH LIBRARY
4600 MA
DETROIT, MI 48210
(313) 224-6481

Flippin' The Game II:

By

Myles and Alethea Ramzee

RJ Publications, LLC

Newark, New Jersey

FEB 2018

The characters and events in this book are fictitious. Any resemblance to actual persons, living or dead is purely coincidental.

RJ Publications
alethearamzee@yahoo.com
www.rjpublications.com
Copyright © 2009 by Myles Ramzee
All Rights Reserved
ISBN 0981777384
978-0981777382

Without limiting the rights under copyright reserved above, no part of this book may be reproduced in any form whatsoever without the prior consent of both the copyright owner and the above publisher of this book.

Printed in the Canada

December 2009

1 2 3 4 5 6 7 8 9 10

FEB 2010

CONELY BRANCH

FLIPPIN THE GAME II

Stand up: The jury's back

A novel by

Alethea & Myles Ramzee

<u>Introduction</u>

I understand the jury. You the reader have rendered your verdict before it is announced. I would like to make a few points to the readers of Flippin The Game part 1.

Yes, it was our intention to entertain our readers and I hope that purpose was achieved. It is important for the readers to know that entertainment wasn't the only purpose of this novel.

In no way, form or fashion did I or my co-author write *Flippin The Game* to glamorize or glorify the sale of drugs, murder, or any criminal act that characters in the story committed. Sadly, these crimes and the lifestyle that come with "The Game" are a reality that some people face and live with, voluntarily and involuntarily, on a daily basis.

There is no glory and glamour when children go hungry living in dirty conditions due to neglect from addicted parents who spend money for food, clothing and other necessities on drugs. These neglected children look at street corner hustlers as role models or neighborhood celebrities. What is so glamorous about these hustlers turning once decent communities into urban war zones resulting in the untimely deaths of innocent children and adults caught in the cross fire of gang warfare?

Am I judging those who have chosen to go down that destructive path? No. I too have gone down that same path only to find out that at the end of the road is a brick wall that I crashed into head first. I went so deep down that path that I couldn't turn back because I had no sense of direction. I didn't know my purpose. I thought my purpose was to go down that destructive path and find a pot of gold at the end of it. I am a witness that there is no pot of gold at the end, only a jail cell or a casket. So to my young readers and those who are on that path or thinking of going down that path, there is nothing glamorous about jail. There is nothing glamorous or cool about your young body being carried by your family in a wooden box to be buried. Mothers shouldn't have to bury their children's bullet riddled bodies. Mothers shouldn't be scared to let their children play in front of the house or in the park because their community is under siege by young hoodlums hell bent on killing each other over streets they don't own or even own a house on.

To those guys or people looking for someone to blame because they feel that it is someone else's fault for the life they chose to live, I'll tell you where you can find that person to blame: they sell mirrors on the commissary and your jail cell should have one over the metal toilet and sink. Enjoy the read.

MYLES RAMZEE

"Honor and loyalty are like newspapers. You read it in the morning on your way to work, then throw it away ten minutes after you bought it………………"

_____ Tank

Prologue

<u>Las Vegas, Nevada</u>

This was it; it was his time, time to erase the blemishes and wounds on the reputation of his family legacy. He could feel the adrenaline rush through his body as he climbed the white picket fence in the backyard of the one story bungalow. Sweat dripped under his black Polo turtleneck from the humid, steamy Vegas night. When his feet hit the grass, he froze momentarily to see if anyone in the house or the house adjacent to the bungalow could hear him. He glared at the windows of both homes waiting to see if lights came on. He didn't have to worry about the neighbor's German shepherd barking, courtesy of the tranquilizer he stuffed in a prime rib steak he tossed over the gate. After about a minute or two the dog was out cold.

Assured that no one heard him, he proceeded towards the back of the home where a sliding glass door led directly into the living room. "I hope she left the door unlocked", he mumbled to himself. Getting to the door, he slowly opened the glass door with a gloved hand. He exhaled, relieved that the woman kept her word and didn't renege on the deal set between them. He glared at the alarm system and read the digital words "system unarmed". He walked carefully through the dark home; almost tip-toeing, thinking the black soft moccasins would make noise on the hardwood floor. He quietly removed his black Glock equipped with a silencer from his black Dickies and found his way to the master bedroom. He knew from the woman who conspired with him to do the job, that only one person would be in the house this particular night. The person he was looking for, that person would also be in a deep drug induced sleep from some pills the woman would slip in his drink, prior to her leaving the home to visit some friends across town. Her only child was at a sleepover at one of her classmate's houses.

He pushed the white double doors to the master bedroom open, and immediately saw the frame of a body under the thick gold colored Versace blankets. "I got you now, you punk bitch", he mumbled with a smile. Entering the room, the plush white carpet felt as if he were going to sink in it. The person under the covers was completely hidden. The oak wood canopy bed sat in the middle of the spacious bedroom with a leather lounge chair beside it. He walked to the bed with the gun pointed at the silhouette, and with his free hand he pulled the blanket back. As he aimed the gun at the man's face, he stood in shock at what he saw. His heart pounded. He was shocked, surprised, and angry at what he was now seeing. The man's face in the bed was contorted as if he saw a ghost before someone blew half of his head all over the oversized gold colored satin pillow. Well, some of the pillow was gold most of it was a dark burgundy from the blood and brain matter that leaked into it. "Motherfucker!" he grunted angrily 'cause obviously someone got to do what he came to do, something he meticulously planned for a long time. Even though it was a good thing that the man got what he deserved, he felt as if he were robbed of the opportunity to get some payback.

He sat on the lounge chair with his head down, the gun still in his hand.

"Who the, this slimy bitch, she knew !" he growled. Suddenly, he stood up and pointed the gun at the corpse. "Might as well get mines too." He squeezed the trigger three times and pumped bullets into the corpse's chest making the body jerk. He walked out of the house the same way he entered. He quietly closed the glass sliding door and walked to the picket fence. Before he could climb the fence he heard a sound that he dreaded, a sound he knew meant shit was about to get crazy. "Freeze F.B.I don't move! Put your hands up now!"

XXXXXXXXXXXXXXXXXXXX

Two hours later
Vegas office of the F.B.I

"I'm going to ask you one more time. Who were you with; we know you didn't act alone!" A stank breath agent yelled to the man, sitting in a metal chair cuffed to a table nailed down to the cement floor.

The cuffed man stared at the camera mounted on the ceiling in a corner of the gray interrogation room. The man smiled into the camera before replying. "I didn't graduate from Quantico. I graduated from the streets of South Philadelphia, that's your job, not mine."

In another office a lieutenant of the U.S Marshals listened on the phone as a superior in Washington D.C barked, "How the hell did this happen? This guy was your responsibility goddamn it!"

"Sir, I know."

"You know shit, Lieutenant. This is inexcusable in this agency. This never happened in the history of this agency's existence, someone is gonna pay for this, and it's gonna cost people jobs!"

The lieutenant dialed a number on his desk phone. When the phone was picked up, he spoke in an agitated tone.

"Did you hear anything from the woman?"

"Yes, she has a solid alibi. She was at the home of one of the agents in charge of her family's protection." There was a long pause from the lieutenant, then a dial tone.

The night after the murder the woman who conspired to kill the man, stood in a public phone booth on the busy, lit up Vegas strip trying to look as inconspicuous as possible. Oversized 70's style shades covered her eyes and half of her face. She couldn't be recognized by anyone who knew her due to the long, silky wig she wore. Her natural dark hair wasn't as dark as the wig, and her Nike Air Max sneakers made her appear shorter than usual. Her usual four inch designer shoes made her look taller then her five foot three inch frame.

She listened pitifully as the voice on the phone whimpered. "So you used me as an alibi, how long have you planned this?"

"That's not the case, baby. I swear," she said while she put her Louis Vuitton backpack down by her feet.

"All of a sudden you're leaving the program... that looks mighty suspicious. You could care less that my job is on the line. I have to go see the lieutenant in the morning. I know I'm gonna lose my job!" The voice on the phone snarled.

"I'm sorry about all this. It's just a coincidence," she lied.

While she talked, she looked nervously up and down the strip trying to spot any cops looking for her. She knew they were suspicious of her even though she had a solid alibi. She didn't wanna be in Vegas just in case the F.B.I cracked the case. She knew from experience that the most treacherous, murderous people can buckle under pressure. She had a strong doubt that the guy who committed the murder would rat her out, but she would rather be safe than sorry.

"I had nothing at all to do with this, I swear on my child," she continued, crossing her fingers as she lied.

The man on the phone sighed. "I'm not sure I believe you. It's all too strange to me." His comment made him second-guess his relationship with her.

He was a U.S. Marshal in charge of protecting her and her family from dangerous men who wanted them dead. Her husband was out of the house a lot, usually gambling at the many casinos along the Vegas strip. He didn't worry about being spotted because plastic surgery did a wonderful job of hiding who he truly was. While he freely paraded around town, the U.S. Marshal spent a lot of time around the wife. Their Scrabble games and long talks over coffee and snacks along with her shopping trips to Rodeo Drive in Cali turned into flirting, then eventually a relationship of sneaky wild sex with her being the initiator of it all. Her sex appeal made it hard for any man to turn a blind eye. Once she put her seduction to work, she usually got her prey caught in her web.

The things she did to a man sexually were something out of a sex fantasy. Once she put her sexual prowess down on the agent, she had him wrapped around her finger. And yes, he is a married man.

"I'm sorry but I have to go," she said.

"So that's it. You just erase what we had and act like it was nothing between us?"

She shook her head in disbelief at his comment. She thought to herself, 'damn I'm good. He couldn't have possibly thought we were a couple. You give a man some pussy, I know this is some real good pussy, and they think they own you. He's married. He thought I was married to a low down snitch. He knows my background, what made him think we could be anything else but a fuck?'

"I won't erase it. I'll keep it close to my heart, bye." She hung up the phone and walked off, away from her short Vegas life forever. Twenty minutes later she boarded a plane to New York to reunite with her husband.

Three thousand miles away on a foggy early morning in Fair Mount Park, Philadelphia a male jogger dressed in a blue hooded sweat shirt and blue Polo sweat pants, answered his Nokia phone as he jogged.

"*As-Salamu Alaykum*" the jogger said in a deep breathing voice.

"We Alaykum Salaam," the voice on the phone replied.

"You got some news I can use?" The jogger asked as he stopped jogging waiting for the black Lincoln town car behind him to stop. He entered the rear of the town car gesturing for the driver to move. Removing the hood from his head, he rubbed his beard.

"The cheese is off the rat trap," the voice on phone replied before hanging up.

The jogger placed his phone on the leather seat and smiled. He patted the driver on the shoulder. "Drive to New York to pick my wife up." The driver nodded his head and sped off exiting the park. The jogger looked out at the foggy Philadelphia morning still smiling. He then mumbled, "One snitch down, one to go."

CHAPTER ONE

MATTHEW FARROW

<u>Deliberation Room</u>

It's easy for these eleven people to send a black man to prison for the rest of his life. With the exception of me and Katherine, (who names a black child Katherine?) the jury is made up of white men and women. They are eager to send Nafiys Muhammad back where they feel every young black male in the ghettoes of America, who hasn't been properly educated because the inner city public school system cares nothing about them, belongs.

Actually, I'm the only black person here. Katherine, a "5'5 petite, Robin Givens look alike is whiter in personality then the country clubbers on this jury. She's suffering from a bad case of plantation psychosis. She is trying her hardest to impress the jury with her uppity, suburban vernacular, her blue contact lenses, expensive clothing and judgmental remarks. "These people try to hide their criminal acts behind legitimate businesses all the time," she said talking out of her nostrils like some whites do, making a squeaky sound. Boy was she annoying. Good thing is, I'm the foreman of this jury and I'll make sure we follow the law to the tee.

"I don't believe the government met its burden on the RICO charge, "I said, causing my caviar eating, golf playing, *Wall Street Journal* reading fellow jurors to stare at me in disbelief. Good thing there weren't any weapons in this room 'cause some of the looks seemed as if they wanted to get rid of another black plague. I grabbed the clear plastic pitcher of water from the long oval shaped conference table cluttered with pieces of scrap paper where notes were taken, Styrofoam cups and other personal items of the jurors. Though the white painted room with nothing on the walls and a gray tiled floor that was over-waxed was large, it seemed smaller due to the space taken up by the many court exhibits and evidence placed on charts. After pouring a cup of water from the pitcher, I took a sip and listened.

"The judge instructed us on the RICO statute that a person doesn't have to commit a murder to be guilty of the RICO charge. If the government proves that the defendant's actions aided in the criminal enterprise then he is guilty." A pale freckle-faced woman probably in her late 30's commented. She was in bad need of a teeth cleaning. Cigarettes and too much coffee made her teeth look like a dirty mop. Other jurors nodded in agreement with her comment. I knew I was going to be the only voice of reason.

"None of the murders that Classon testified to occurred after Mr. Muhammad met the Classon brothers. They were all before he met Jerry Classon in prison."

"The question is," Katherine joined in with her annoying voice, "Do we believe Jerry Classon? Personally I feel he shouldn't get a break. He should get as much time as anyone else, but why would Classon lie?"

"Obviously so he won't spend the rest of his life in jail," I shot back. It doesn't take a rocket scientist to figure out that one, but I'm not dealing with rocket scientists or the likes with this jury. I'm dealing with a bunch of tight ass white folks whose biggest worries are property taxes and the stock market crashing, not the lives of children and people living in the forgotten ghettoes of America.

"Mr. Muhammad's indictment in this case is crimes committed from the time he got out of prison until his arrest."

"What about the phone call and the conversation with his friend about the hold up in Philadelphia and the robbery of the drug courier who was bringing drugs to Mr. Muhammad…"

I had to cut the tight suit wearing, over tanned, blond haired, spoiled rich kid off.

"There was no proof that the drugs were for Muhammad."

"That goes back to what Katherine said," Gloria blurted out. She was an attractive Sarah Jessica Parker type, you know the type of white woman who lives in an Upper West Side brownstone by herself, and independent woman who dates men for casual sex then gets rid of them when they become too attached. "Do we believe Classon or not? If we don't believe him then the only direct evidence we have on Mr. Muhammad is the gun they found during the raid."

Gloria had a point. The phone call and the conversation in the car with his friend were just two guys discussing something they heard on the streets. I admired her willingness to be open-minded about the whole situation. She paid attention to detail, a woman who listened more then she talked, a rare attribute for women.

Another good thing about being on the jury is that our verdict isn't just based on what I and these eleven so called peers of Nafiys Muhammad think. The verdict actually comes from you, the reader. You read part one of this saga and the verdict is in.

Let's get to it.

CHAPTER TWO

<u>HONORABLE BOYMAN TRAUB</u>

"Jury foreman, please hand the bailiff the verdict."

This is one of those trials where I have reasonable doubt on a few of the charges, but my personal feelings have no place in this proceeding. After thanking the bailiff for handing me the verdict I looked at the results then out to the packed Brooklyn courtroom. You could feel the tension in the air mixed in with the smell of wood and the scent of oils worn by the Muslims in attendance. The defendant, Nafiys Muhammad, sat next to his attorney; the flamboyant Mr. Shabazz---composed and focused. Most of the spectators you could tell were edgy in anticipation, and of course, nervous.

Reading the verdict, I wasn't surprised by what I was reading. After three days of deliberation I guess this is what it boils down to.

"Jury foreman, is this a true and correct verdict?" I asked.

"Yes your honor."

"Will the defendant please rise? I'll advise everyone in the courtroom to remain seated and avoid any outbursts. If my warning is not heeded you will be held in contempt."

Putting my spectacles on, I read the verdict.
"On the charge under the RICO statute, it is the verdict of this jury that Mr. Nafiys Muhammad is not guilty."

"On count number two, section 102, interstate trafficking of a controlled substance, the jury is hopelessly deadlocked.

"On count number three, criminal possession of a weapon; it is the verdict of this jury that Mr. Nafiys Muhammad is not guilty. As for count 2 it is up to the government to decide within 45 days if they will retry the defendant on count 2 of the indictment. Court is adjourned."

CHAPTER 3

<u>NAFIYS</u>

Not Guilty, not guilty. Those were words that made a brother like me feel like he just bust his first nut. I hugged my lawyer so hard I almost squeezed the life out of him.

"We did it Nafiys!" Shabazz managed to say while trying to breathe. Letting him go, I turned to face my family and friends with the goofiest smile they probably ever saw from me. The first person I made eye contact with was my woman, Ryan. She had tears in her eyes while she held my son in her hands, my beautiful son, Allahu Akbar!

I still had that one charge hanging over my head. It wasn't as serious as the RICO charge but my freedom was still not guaranteed. The U.S. Marshals led me out of the courtroom. I waved to my family and my son. I mouthed to Ryan "I love you" as I was escorted out of the courtroom to a bullpen.

"The judge will give you bail. Even if the government opposes it, you will get bail and probably home monitoring," Shabazz, my attorney said.

"I'll post bail, just give it back when you hit the town."

"What do you think about this charge, you think they will retry me?" I asked nervously.

I have faith in Shabazz's skills, but the government ain't nothing to play with. When they want you, they will find a way to get you. There's nothing more powerful than the U.S government, except Allah.

I could tell by Shabazz's expression that he knew they would try and hang me on the charge. "Yeah they will, but I can beat this. I wonder why they were deadlocked on that charge," Shabazz thought for a second. Sitting on the plastic visiting booth chair with his arms folded in deep thought; he shrugged his shoulders, "Juries are like women, you can never figure them."

I would have to wait a week for my bail hearing. In the mean time, I was taken back to the M.C.C., Corey was already shipped to the Atlanta penitentiary. He'll be alright over there. I know a lot of real dudes down there and I'll put the word out that Corey is cool. I can't front, Corey started getting funny style on me. First he would be stressed out about the whole thing, then he wants to sit around and tell war stories to niggas he don't know from a can of paint. To make matters worse, some people from the street magazine called *Streets is Watching* interviewed him and he starts yapping like he's not trying to appeal his case.

XXXXXXXXXXXXXXXXXXXX

BEFORE THE VERDICT:

"Yo, Na, them people from the *Streets is Watching* magazine wrote me. They said they can get clearance to interview me for their mag. They are doing a story on the Southside of Jamaica Queens and its street legends, Corey said excitedly as we walked the yard. All the while I'm thinking to myself that this dude seems like he is actually entertaining the thought of doing the interview.

"What you thinking 'bout talking to them people?" I had to ask. Corey lit a cigarette looking away from me towards a group of dudes with their orange jumpsuits tied around their waists playing hand ball. After lighting the cigarette, he shrugged his shoulders. "I'm not going to talk about my case, just about growing up on the Southside and the old stories." I stopped walking, giving Corey a skeptical look. "C'mon Cee, you ain't talking to no fool, baby, you know what they wanna hear. You read the magazine before, all niggas do is talk about what they locked up for and what they had." "If they ask me about my case, I'm a check them," Corey shot back, adding a little gangsta attitude in his tone trying to sound convincing.

I wasn't at the interview, but for some reason I didn't believe him. I just hope he isn't foolish enough to incriminate himself or anyone else who escaped detection by the federal government.

CHAPTER 4

<u>RYAN</u>

If I wasn't in this courtroom, I would've jumped up screaming Allah Akbar, (God is great) not guilty! I'm pretty sure he will beat the other charge if this prosecutor chooses to retry the case, until then my baby is going to get bail and come home to me and his son.

It felt good to see Nafiys smile the way he did when the verdict was read. I can't say that for some of the families of the deceased victims that Class and Corey were responsible for. I heard the grunts and gasps from the opposite side of the courtroom, along with evil stares from people I never saw in my life. I mouthed "I love you too" as Nafiys was led from the courtroom.

Outside of the courthouse is where I let out how I felt, of course my best friend, Kwanda, was there for me. At first, I was angry at Kwanda for what she supposedly did to Trish and Class. Trish told me that the Feds said Kwanda tipped them off about Class, Kwanda denied it in tears. "I would never do that to my friends, Ryan, I swear on my life and my nieces and nephews' lives!" She cried to me over the phone after I spoke to Trish. She called me from God only knows where, but couldn't tell me.

"I'm just telling you what Trish said."

"If that's true, why didn't I do it to you, why would I just pick her?" Kwanda asked, making her point. We were all close and Kwanda had no reason at all to do that to Trish. Maybe the Feds were using that as a tactic to scare Trish. What I don't understand is, why Trish would be mad at

Kwanda for supposedly snitching, but her man is the biggest rat of them all.

I hugged Kwanda outside the courthouse and almost screamed. "My baby is coming home, Kwanda!"

We hugged and bounced up and down. "I'm so happy for you Ryan. You deserve that."

Hearing my baby cry, I turned to see Nafiys' cousin, Tamara, ready to hand him to me. Tamara was a pretty, light-skinned 18 year-old with a real ghetto attitude. She was the total opposite of Nafiys. She was loud and obnoxious and you could tell by her dull complexion and dark lips that she spent most of her day smoking weed.

"This boy is having a fit Ryan. Please take him," Tamara said with her cocky Philly accent. The last thing on her mind was holding the baby. She wanted to flaunt her body with some Akademik jeans that were so tight, you could practically see her veins. Nafiys' friends, all dressed expensively with different styles of urban apparel, flossing jewelry that brought light to the cloudy Brooklyn afternoon, paid her no mind.

My nerves were finally able to cool out. Before the verdict I couldn't stop shaking. When I got a call from Nafiys the night before, he really made me edgy with his pessimism.

"If I'm found guilty, don't worry Ryan, you're always going to be taken care of. You and my son will have the best. I know and understand you will want to move on and…"

Of course I cut him off immediately; I wasn't tryna get into that type of talk.

"Don't talk like that Nafiys. Allah forbids, if they find you guilty, there won't be no moving on. You're my life partner. Life--you hear me?"

I'm so glad this is over, well the worst of it is. At least he is not facing life no more.

"C'mon Kwanda lets go celebrate," I said after grabbing my son from Tamara.

"What are we going to do?" Kwanda asked curiously.

"Girl what do we usually do when we celebrate?"

"Shop?" Kwanda asked as if she were confused.

"You know it."

CHAPTER 5

<u>KWANDA</u>

I'm so happy for Ryan. She deserves to have Nafiys back home where they can live their lives happily ever after. Nafiys is a good man for Ryan. He makes her happy, and he's lucky to have a loyal woman like Ryan. Since we were kids Ryan has always been a loyal, trustworthy girl. She's a girlfriend that any chic can trust around her man. I can't say that for Trish. Now don't get me wrong I love Trish like a sister, but when it comes to men, Trish becomes another person and it's been like that for years.

XXXXXXXXXXXXXXXXXXXXXX

<u>1983</u>

<u>Martin Luther King H.S</u>

The first official day of school is the day everyone shows up in their best apparel. If your gear wasn't up to par, you might as well not exist. For freshmen such as me, this was the day that could make or break my reputation. Martin Luther King High School was a school different from most schools in Manhattan.

In Harlem, the kids in the school were from Harlem just like schools around the city. You had to go to the school in your zone. King was different, kids from all over New York City attended, so you had to always be at your best at King. Your section of the city's rep was on the line. For us Harlem kids, our biggest competitors were kids from

Brooklyn. There were a lot of Brooklyn kids at King. The majority of them were troublemakers who got kicked out of Brooklyn schools and came to King. And of course, they brought their Brooklyn pride with them. As far as dressing, we Harlem kids had that on lock. There were no competitors in that department. Brooklyn kids gave us a run for our money 'cause the majority of them were boosters who raided stores all over Manhattan for the latest gear.

Harlem people are known for style. A lot of the boys from Harlem were hustlers who showed up to school in fly cars and clothes and flashed wads of money to get the girls' attention. Some of the Harlem girls were these guys' girlfriends who also stayed fly cause guys don't like to be seen with a girl who wasn't up to par, so they spoiled the girls with gifts of clothes, jewelry and if the guy was a real big money getter, girls would even get cars as gifts. Then you had girls from Harlem who had brother, father, uncles or cousins who made money on the streets and those girls didn't need nothing from no guy who hustled. They got it all from their relatives, and Trish was the Queen when it came to that. In fact, she was the Queen of Martin Luther King High School. Let her tell it, she was the Queen of New York.

Standing in front of the school talking to Ryan, we were interrupted by a black four door Mercedes Benz that pulled up. All the kids who were standing there modeling their new clothes all stared as Trish stepped out of the Benz from the passenger side wearing black leather snake skin boots that came up to her calves, black Sergio Valente jeans with a white silk button down under a white waist length fur coat. Her hair was done up in a mushroom style. Gold hoop earrings reached down to her neck, and gold bracelets almost covered up to her elbow. Trish was fly and she carried herself like she knew it.

"Wassup ya'll," Trish greeted us, almost posing like a model at a photo shoot once she noticed the stares from awe struck and envious kids. At the time, Ryan's father was a successful real estate investor who owned a couple of brownstones in Harlem, and my pops was a Dominican hustler who spoiled me whenever he wasn't in jail or hiding out in Santo Domingo. Ryan and I dressed the part, no fur coats or lots of jewelry, but we could be seen in name brands like Louis Vuitton, Gucci and the like. I guess that was what brought the three of us together. We were from Harlem and we dressed better than the average girls. I know how superficial it sounds, but that's how most people become friends, they have something in common.

We hung out together in school and after school. We were inseparable. We were teenage girls who liked to dance, talk about the latest clothes and of course, boys. Ryan wasn't into boys like me and Trish. She was more of a bookworm, but she dressed fly, so me and Trish liked her. I could say I was the prettiest and more developed physically than my two partners. Because I was, that got me lots of attention from boys, but it was Trish who got the best picks. I guess a lot of the cute boys wanted to be seen with her to boost their rep. She was Bish's niece, one of the biggest hustlers and gangstas past 110th Street. If I became interested in a boy in school or in the neighborhood and shared it with Trish, a day or two later she would be hugged up with him. I don't know if it was out of spite just to show me that it didn't matter that I had the better body and looks, she was still Queen or if she just wanted the guy. The one thing I learned was not to tell Trish if I liked a boy. Then, there was Rick.

Rick came to King after being kicked out of three schools in the Bronx. He was a cute Puerto Rican boy a year older than me who had soft curly, hair big brown eyes and lips that looked like they were soft as baby skin. His teeth were white and perfect and he dressed fly. They say his father was one of the biggest dope dealers in the Bronx. All the girls at King wanted him, especially after one afternoon incident when a group of Brooklyn kids tried to rob him for his leather bomber jacket. Rick stood fearless in front of the three Brooklyn kids and said "Ya'll going have to knock me out to get this. If ya'll don't, I'm a knock ya'll out one by one," and he did. Rick's father taught him how to box when he was eight years old. Nobody ever messed with Rick again. I wanted him bad.

Every time I saw him in the hallway, I made sure he saw me. I started wearing tighter pants so he could see my thick frame. I kept lip gloss so my full lips could glow and I smiled at him a lot. I even chewed gum seductively when he was around and it worked.

"What's your name pretty?" Rick said with his deep sexy Bronx accent. When he licked his lips, my nipples got hard and I felt embarrassed cause I felt naked as they bulged against my white body suit. I saw his eyes undress me as I leaned against my locker. "Kwanda, why?" I said trying to sound annoyed and disinterested. I didn't want to look as if I were desperate, something I learned from Trish.

"Dam girl why you so hostile, I'm just tryna get to meet the prettiest girl in the school, that's all." I couldn't stop myself from blushing though I tried hard, but looking at this beautiful specimen in front of me, I couldn't resist.

"I'm not being hostile, I'm just tired, that's all," I lied. He told me his name and where he was from. After school, he took me to McDonalds, and paid for my meal. We exchanged numbers and that night I spoke to Rick for hours until my mother yelled for me to get off the phone. I have a loud mother, so I quickly hung up, but I was hooked on Rick.

Rick came to my house one weekend to take me to the movies. As we walked out of my family's brownstone, I saw Trish walking up the crowded block towards us. I wanted so badly for her not to see us, but the wide eyed expression on her face spoiled any thought of me and him not being spotted. Trish acted as if she didn't notice Rick in school. She wanted him to approach her; she was "The Queen." Rick didn't give her a second look when he saw her in the hall. I know that pissed her off.

"Hey Kwanda, what you up to?" Trish asked with a fake smile avoiding eye contact with Rick. I took a hard swallow before answering.

"Rick and I are going to the movies."

"Oh, I thought we were going to hang out," Trish said. I had no idea what she was talking about. I was with her all day and there was no plan to hang out. Rick looked at his gold watch then gave me the "we got to get going" look. "I'll call you tomorrow Trish." Rick and I walked off, leaving Trish staring at our backs. Rick and I caught the Matinee and we barely watched the movie. We kissed almost through the whole thing. We ate at Red Lobster, and at our booth, Rick questioned me about Trish.

"I heard that friend of yours is Bish's niece," Rick said chewing on some fried shrimp. I was a little surprised. Rick being from the Bronx I didn't think he knew who Bish was.

"You know who Bish is?" Rick replied.

I knew Bish was big, but I didn't think his name was big all over the city. I guess I was wrong.

"Yup that's Bish's niece."

Before the day ended with Rick and I having sex at his mother's Bronx apartment, on her bed, Rick asked a lot of questions about Trish. It bothered me a little because I wanted him to ask me about me, but once we laid in bed naked and Rick filled my insides up with his throbbing manhood, I forgot all about our conversation and gripped and scratched his light brown skin leaving long scratches on his back. This was my second sexual experience and the best out of the two. We left his mother's sheets soak and wet with sweat and sex juice.

I walked in King that Monday morning to find Trish or Ryan. I was running late that day, on my way to class the halls were empty because all the kids were in class. As I passed the girls bathroom I heard a laugh that sounded familiar. I recognized Trish's laugh. I pushed the bathroom door open and my heart dropped into my leather boots. There was Trish hugging and kissing my man. The guy I was beginning to fall in love with, Rick with his hands gripping Trish's ass placing his tongue down her throat. They both looked at me once they heard the door open.

"Hey Kwanda wassup," Trish said hugging Rick even tighter around his waist. "Wassup Kwanda," Rick said nonchalantly.

"Yo ya'll is foul. Fuck ya'll!" I growled and walked out of the school. It felt like my heart stayed at school while my body walked through Manhattan as if I were a derelict. To make matters worse, I was picked up by truant cops and taken back to school. The cops walked me to the principal's office, the walk felt like the green mile. Everybody was looking at me like I was a new inmate being led to his cell with a big mean cellmate who had a shank. The inmate was Rick and he stabbed me in the heart.

I didn't talk to Trish for weeks, until Ryan brought us together at our lunch table and begged for us to make up. "C'mon ya'll, we been friends for too long to let some boy come between us. Please don't do this, he played both of ya'll. Look at him now." Ryan pointed to another lunch table where Rick had his arms around a pretty Puerto Rican girl. He was whispering in her ear and she was smiling from ear to ear. Ryan was right, I knew Trish since elementary school. I couldn't let that two-timing animal break us up.

"I'm sorry, Kwanda. I didn't know you had feelings for him. I swear," Trish said with a sad look on her face.

"I'm sorry for not talking to you about it," I replied. We hugged and promised never to let a man come between us. Was it an empty promise? You figure it out.

XXXXXXXXXXXXXXXXXXXXX

2004

"So what are we going to do? I'm tired of the secret love affair. I'm tired of sharing too.

"I got you Kwanda. You know me and her is almost over, gimme some time to work things out."

"Well, make it quick, nigga, 'cause your mines now and I don't wanna have to hurt nobody."

"Let's not talk about violence now. Let's continue our exercise."

Damn this nigga dick almost goes down my throat. My jaws be sore as hell but it's worth it. "You like it um-hum, gimme that nut. I wanna taste you now Class…"

CHAPTER 6

<u>Nasir Shabazz esquire</u>

After getting Nafiys out on $100,000 bail, we met at Masjid in the Germantown section of Philly. The first thing he did after greeting me in peace was hand me a brown paper bag filled with cash.

"That's a buck fifty, the fifty for your trouble, feel me?" Nafiys smiled. An extra fifty gees, that's Nafiys for you, always the generous one.

After pulling Nafiys to the side, away from his large bearded menacing body guard, we entered a room designated for men to remove their shoes before entering the large prayer room.

"The U.S. attorney is going to retry you. I've asked for a continuance from the set date in order to prepare." Nafiys sighed at the news I relayed to him. The government wants Nafiys and black men like him off the streets. A person under their watchful eyes isn't supposed to beat his case, especially a black man, regardless of his innocence. They want people to believe that it's impossible for a former criminal from the ghetto to go straight. If he becomes successful legally there has to be something criminal that got him his start to the legal life. This notion is evident in the music business, particularly in hip hop genre. Ex-cons trying their hand at legitimacy become targets of the F.B.I. immediately. These men last longer on the streets selling drugs than they do trying to become productive members of society, conspiracy theory?

"I'll postpone this trial as long as I can. Until then, stay low. Disappear as much as possible because they will be watching your every move," I warned him.

After our time at the mosque we went to Nafiys' Upper Darby home to celebrate. Ryan and a couple of sisters from the Germantown mosque prepared an abundance of Halal and soul food. The house smelled wonderful from the food and incense that permeated the spacious two story Mediterranean style home. The polished Brazilian wood floor was covered in expensive Oriental rugs. Mixed with a Spanish style décor, the large terrarium with its beautiful floral interior that hosted a couple of small lizards stood out in the immaculate home. Nafiys sat down on a large chocolate suede couch and adjusted the ankle monitor.

"This jawn is annoying," he complained as I sat next to him.

"One of the prices of the game, Fiys," a deep voiced, slim light-skinned brother with no facial hair, wearing a black Kofi over his bald head said.

Nafiys looked at the guy who appeared to be in his early 20's with an annoyed expression. "Allah gave you two eyes, two ears and one mouth. That means observe and listen more than you talk." The young guy looked embarrassed as he stared down at his feet."

"Will they call this clown to testify again?" Nafiys asked after placing his black slacks over his ankle monitor.

"I suppose, all they have is him saying that drugs were being trafficked between New York and Philly. Lil' Butchie is hiding out, so it's your word against Class. I think I can get Lil' Butchie's statement read into the record once I prove he is unavailable," I said to Nafiys.

In a way I hope Lil' Butchie stays on the run at least until Nafiys' trial is over. If they catch him now he might wanna make a deal to get out of his charges. Plus, Lil'

Butchie is a wolf in sheep's clothing, a snake if I ever saw one. There is so much I want to tell Nafiys about Lil' Butchie, but right now isn't the time. If I was to tell him now what I know, there is no telling what Nafiys would do. I don't want him to jeopardize his freedom, at the same time he is my friend and I'm caught between a rock and a hard place. Every time I think of Lil' Butchie's betrayal, it really gets my blood boiling and I want to kill him myself, but Allah is the best of planners. What he has planned for people like Lil' Butchie is a million times worse than what I or any man's bullet or knife could give him. I wish what I knew wouldn't have dropped into my lap the way it did.

XXXXXXXXXXXXXXXXXXXXXX

"They arrested my son. He needs you now. They got him at the district talking bout some damn murders. Mr. Shabazz, help him!"

I was awakened out of a deep sleep by the ringing of my cell phone only to answer it and listen as one of my client's mother screamed frantically into my ear.

"Ms. Malone, calm down and tell me what happened," I said half asleep in a groggy voice. I slipped from under my silk sheets trying not to wake my wife. Once I got in the hall after putting on my black cotton robe, I continued.

"I can't understand you if you're screaming Ms Malone."

"The cops bust down the door and arrested him for murder. I think he's at 8th and Race."

I washed up and quickly got dressed to head downtown, wondering to myself what murder they were trying to put on Chris now. Every month they hauled this dude down to the district trying to put an unsolved North Philadelphia homicide on him. They never stick. Chris does have a murderous reputation that stretched back to the early and late 80's, but if he did them, he never had another person witness it, or they were too scared to say anything. On a few occasions witnesses disappeared. When I got into the interrogation room, Chris wasn't his normal calm and collective self. His face was drenched in sweat making his dark skin shine and he looked scared to death. And the worst of it all, he was running his mouth.

I introduced myself, which I really didn't have to do. Every cop in Philly knows who I am and I know they hate me. They feel I defend the worst of the worst and help them get out of long jail terms and get deals for criminals. It's not my job to form an opinion on guilt or innocence. My job is to make sure people get a fair trial, something guaranteed by the Constitution. So don't be angry with me, be angry with the forefathers of this great nation, I immediately told Chris: "Stop talking Chris, now!"

The detectives didn't give me the usual looks of disgust for giving my client the best advice a lawyer could give in a situation like this. Instead, they smiled and handed me a waiver that Chris signed. Then I saw some papers in front of Chris that he already filled with his own words.

"Shabazz they got me. I got to help myself out of this shit," Chris cried. I picked the statement up and read it.

He told the police about a few unsolved homicides that he was either the killer or some how involved in. One of the murders stuck out to me when I saw Lil' Butchie's name on the statement. When I read what Lil' Butchie was involved in, I almost tore the statement up and threw it at Chris. To make the situation worse, one of the detectives says "That's sad Mr. Shabazz. Mr. Muhammad's best friend set his older brother up. I think we have a serious conflict of interest. You can't represent Chris here while you're representing the guy who's brother Chris killed."

They were right. I didn't want to ruin Nafiys' homecoming celebration, so I was going to tell him when the time was right. The right time, I decided would be before the trial. I didn't feel it would be right to tell him after the trial. If he got convicted, which I doubt, I wouldn't wanna stress him out in jail on top of the stress of being locked up. Whenever he came to my office to discuss the trial, I would tell him.

Chapter 7

<u>Class</u>

I guess I wasn't as believable to Nafiys' jury as I was to Corey's. Hey, I wasn't testifying to make sure these guys go away forever. I was doing it so I wouldn't go away forever. Think what ya'll wanna think. I did what I had to do to stay home with my family. It's a good thing Nafiys came up off some serious charges. The messed up thing about it is I have to testify again. I'm tired of this shit for real

I was just getting dug in to my new home out here in Milwaukee. The Feds got me and Trish a nice tan, one story home situated on the corner of a quiet block in a secluded section of the city. Coco liked the house, especially the big well manicured backyard that she could run free in. The home came with George Smith furniture, Poggenpohl kitchen cabinets and granite countertop. Ya'll don't know about that, that's classy stuff right there.

The agent in charge of me and my family's witness protection called me a day after the verdict telling me I would have to testify again whenever Nafiys went back to trial. They doubt the U.S Attorney would offer a plea bargain. I guess they knew Fiys wouldn't plead out, especially after beating the serious R.I.C.O joint. I wouldn't plead out if I was him either. They weren't going to offer probation, and they wanted Fiys bad.

I didn't wanna put up with the stress of staying in the barracks protected by U.S. Marshals with them constantly watching over me. The stress of cross examination and stares from spectators that read "die snitch" were overwhelming. What really stressed me out is when my mother mouthed to me during my brother's trial "Why?" If I could answer her, this is what she would've found out.

XXXXXXXXXXXXXXXXXXXXXXX

2000

I wanted so badly to stop fucking Kwanda, but that pussy is good as a muthafucka. Mentally she really has nothing going for her, but physically, damn! I knew I had to stop dealing with her when she became emotionally attached. I just had to find a way of breaking it to her without her going crazy and running her mouth to Trish.

"So what's next, Class?" Kwanda asked as we both lay naked at the Ramada inn near J.F.K airport. I was trying to catch my breath after two straight hours of nonstop sucking and fucking. She laid her sweaty head on my chest rubbing my manhood at the same time.

"What's next about what?" My question caused her to suck her teeth. "Us, don't act stupid, Class." I knew exactly what she meant. I just had to give myself some time to say the right thing.

"We good," is all I could come up with. Hopefully she understood that meant keep things the way they were, on the low or we had to stop. She raised her head looking me in the eyes. Damn, she is a pretty thing. Her titties bounced on my chest and the softness of her skin caused my manhood to throb.

"What is that supposed to mean, that you'll be my man? That you love me and you're going to marry me one day?"

Whoa what the...where did all that come from? This girl done lost her marbles. Is she serious? Does she actually expect me to just dump Trish, my girl and her so called best friend for her? How would that play out?

"You don't care about Trish's feelings, Kwanda?" That question caused her to bow her head as if she didn't know what to say. Surprisingly she started to suck on my chest making her way down to my bulging dick, taking it into her warm mouth. After about ten minutes of fellatio I exploded in her mouth. After swallowing all of me, she smiled and said "Does that answer your question."

The next morning after we ate breakfast in bed, Kwanda, dropped a bomb on me. "Class, I have to tell you something. Something that I feel you should know." Her tone sounded like a matter of life and death. "My cousin and this nigga, Lam, from around my way were talking bout a robbery they did for Corey in Philly."

I almost knocked my plate of fried eggs and home fries off of the bed "What?" I barked. Kwanda looked fearful as she continued.

"I heard my cousin tell Lam that Corey wanted to rob his brother's man in Philly and make it seem like the Philly dude was behind it. He said he committed the robbery, but Corey was a slimy nigga." I don't know what made me do it. It's like I had no control over myself, like something possessed my body and made me slap the cold shit out of Kwanda.

"You lying bitch. Get yo clothes on. I'm taking you home!"

Kwanda was in shock, tears started rolling down her cheeks.

"I swear to God, Class I'm telling the truth."

"Shut yo fucking mouth. You don't have to take that route to get me to make you my girl."

"I swear Cl--!" I cut her off by raising my hand to slap her again. She curled up in the corner of the room. I threw her clothes at her "Get dressed we're outta here."

I didn't even drop her off at home. I took her to the Long Island Railroad and told her to go home by train. She cried and begged me to believe and forgive her. "Get out of my car and get yo shit together."

When she stepped out of the Benz, I sped off. As I was driving on the Conduit towards the Southside I thought about what Kwanda told me. How did she know about that robbery? I know Trish runs her mouth to her friends, but she didn't know about that. I know damn well Fiys didn't tell Ryan, so how the...Corey wouldn't snake me like that. Kwanda was tryna find a way to get back at Corey for hitting and running on her, that was it. I never mentioned it to Corey; my denial got the best of me. Plus, what would I do if it were true. I can't kill my own brother. If I was to tell Fiys, I couldn't let him do anything to my brother. I just had to chalk it up and keep my business with Nafiys away from Corey. It's a dirty game.

XXXXXXXXXXXXXXXXX

"Class, pick up the phone!" Trish yelled from our master bedroom interrupting me from playing my brand new PlayStation 3. I grabbed the cordless. I knew it could only be the agent in charge of our protection. I didn't give anyone the number and I know Trish didn't. None of Coco's teachers would be calling in the summer. Why would a teacher from Headstart call anyway?

I placed my hand in my white cotton robe and answered the phone after pausing my game of Madden.

"Hello." The voice on the other end was the voice of the agent. What he said was news I didn't need to hear. Not now!

"Your mother is in the hospital, she had a stroke."

CHAPTER 8

<u>TRISH</u>

I'm picturing Ryan's face when she was in the courtroom hearing those not guilty verdicts. I know she probably got lock jaw from the smile that she couldn't control. She's probably still smiling now. I'm happy for her. If anybody deserve s to be happy with their man, it's Ryan.

As far as Kwanda, she denied telling the cops about Class' stash, she said they could've gotten her name off one of the wire taps. She swore on everything she loved that she didn't say anything. I don't know if I believe her, but it doesn't matter anyway, it's done. How could I be mad at her for being a snitch and still deal with Class? In a way I'm mad at Class. I lost respect for him in a lot of ways. How could he do that to his own brother? My lack of respect for him helped ease the guilty feelings I was having about lying to him about Coco being his daughter and cheating on him. I don't feel so bad, for Coco yes, for Class--hell no. I don't wanna lie to Coco, but how do I explain to her that the guy she thought was her father isn't, and that her real father doesn't believe he is her father?

I thought Lil' Butchie was better than that. I know I sprung it on him unexpectedly, but he knows he hit it raw a few times. He couldn't resist, this pussy is too good. Come to find out, the nigga been lying to me about a few things. I never mentioned the lies to 'cause it didn't matter. A good fuck is all I wanted from his ass.

XXXXXXXXXXXXXXXXXXXX

<u>2001</u>

The Harlem funeral parlor was packed to capacity. Everybody from Harlem to California showed up to pay respects to Bish Parker. Every car you can name parked and double parked in front of the parlor for almost 3 blocks. My uncle was loved by many by all. He looked good though. They did a good job cleaning him up and dressing him in a tailored black silk suit. There were so many floral ornaments some had to be removed to make room for mourners.

Most of the mourners were ex-cons who did time with Bish in various federal penitentiaries across the country, from old timers to young muscular guys from different parts of the country. Surprisingly, there were even a few Mexicans there paying respects to Bish.

When it was time for people to say their last words, there were a lot of dangerous looking men in tears expressing their love and pain. The mysterious lady who showed up to kiss Bish and leave was the highlight of the funeral. Some old timers from Harlem spoke of the old days with Bish and how he was "smarter and wiser than any Harlem legend they'd ever encountered in a lifetime."

Nafiys and his crew showed up fashionably late. There was Lil' Butchie looking good as hell in a blue three piece Versace suit. I whispered to Ryan who sat next to me in the second row,"There's the Virginia lover now all decked in blue." Ryan looked over at Nafiys and his crew. After smiling at Nafiys, she whispered to me "Butchie is from Philly, girl. He grew up with Nafiys." I waved it off as if I didn't care, but my blood started to boil. Did he think I was an average ho you dick and split on. Oh hell no! Why did he lie? That's a dumb question when it comes to men, it's like asking why dogs bite, it's in their nature.

During the service, Lil' Butchie acted as if he didn't see me, like I didn't exist. I understand we had to keep this on the low but damn, at least acknowledge me with a nod or smile. Even when I was able to get close to him when Ryan went over to Nafiys outside the parlor, Class was still inside and Nafiys was talking to Ryan, he could've spoken to me.

"Hey Butchie," I whispered. To my utter disgust he just walked away. I wanted to pick up something and throw it at him, I held myself together, though. Anyway, he made it up to me by taking me to South Beach and blowing my back out in a five star hotel.

Kwanda expressed to me that I was playing myself getting that deeply involved with Lil' Butchie. She's always contradicting herself 'cause when I first told her, she was excited for me, but jealousy always gets the best of her. It's been like that since we were young.

XXXXXXXXXXXXXXXXXXX

Christmas 1977

"Stop spoiling that girl, Bish. She's got enough toys for every kid on Saint Nicholas Avenue," my mother told Bish after he walked in our apartment dressed in a blood red three piece pinstriped suit with black gators to match his black gator skinned belt and a Santa Claus hat on his head. He was carrying a large white cotton laundry bag filled with toys for me.

With Bish, it was Christmas everyday for me, anything I wanted he got. When I saw his diamond pinky ring for the first time, I pointed to it and said, "Uncle Bish I want a diamond ring." I didn't know what Uncle Bish or the white man in the jewelry shop were talking about, both of them holding diamonds in their hand looking at them through some type of magnifying glass.

"This is a "D" right here. It's slightly flawed," Uncle Bish said as he looked at the diamond for almost a minute.

"How good is your cut?"

"It will still be "VV" once I cut and make the earrings," the white man answered. Uncle Bish removed a wad of cash from his pocket and handed it to the white man. The white man didn't even count it. He placed it in his pocket and smiled.

"I'll send them uptown tomorrow morning".

"Right on," Bish said then grabbed my little hand and we walked out. The next morning I was awakened by my mother standing over me with a small velvet box in her hand.

"Get up and get dressed. We got to go get your ears pierced. Look what your uncle bought you." My mother opened the box and the room lit up from the sparkle of the 2 karat diamond stud earrings. My mother made sure that I wore my white fox fur the day my ears were pierced and my diamond earrings were placed in my earlobes.

Kwanda lived down the hall from us and when I got home I went to her house to play with her dolls. When her mother answered the door to let me in, she commented on my earrings. "Oooh mommy these are so nice!" Then she yelled in Spanish to Kwanda to come see my earrings. Kwanda came running and the look on her face said it all. She was jealous. Kwanda had a lot of toys and clothing from her father whenever he wasn't in jail or in his country. He stayed away for lengths of time so Kwanda would go through droughts of not getting gifts. This was one of those times. Kwanda started a fight with me that day over the dolls we were playing with. When I was combing one of the dolls' hair, she complained I was doing it wrong. "You're messing her hair up. You don't know what you're doing 'cause your hair is bad." Her calling my hair bad hurt my feelings. Kwanda figured she had something over me that she would throw in my face out of her being jealous of things I had. Kwanda had long pretty hair and of course I had kinky hair. I had yet to get a perm. My mother kept my hair in big box braids with berets. Then, Kwanda over stepped her boundary and snatched the doll out of my hand, yanking my arm damn near out of its socket. I grabbed her ponytail and tried to yank her hair off her head. "Oww, get off of me!" she yelled. She was trying to grab my hands, but I held on with one and begin punching her on top of her head. "Mommy!" Kwanda yelled and started swinging. None of her punches hit me.

"Break it up. What are ya'll fighting for!" Kwanda's mother yelled. She grabbed me by my arm, pulling me off Kwanda.

"She was messing my doll's hair up." Kwanda screamed.

"No I didn't. She didn't want me to do the doll's hair," I shot back. Kwanda's mother laughed at us.

"Why can't you play nicely? Don't let me come back in here 'cause I'm not going to be nice.

I noticed every time I got something new, me and Kwanda started fighting. It's funny how the following year, 1978, when my Uncle Bish got locked up that me and Kwanda's fights came to an end. Also, that year her father came back from wherever he was and Kwanda's drought was over. Fortunately for me, Uncle Bish left my mother a lot of money and some of his friends gave me money to get what I wanted. Unfortunately, my Uncle was sentenced to life.

I never met my father and I was told he was dead. After Uncle Bish got locked up, rumors circulated around Harlem that my father and a guy named Ricky Barns snitched on Uncle Bish. When I asked my mother, she told me to ignore what I heard. "Don't listen to rumors baby.

Your daddy is dead." I wrote Uncle Bish a letter asking him about the rumors. He told me don't believe them. My Uncle's words were gold.

XXXXXXXXXXXXXXXXXX

After I finished bathing Coco, I carried her out with a purple beach towel around her. Class had just gotten plastic surgery. He was still nice looking, but not as handsome as he used to be. Around the house, I still called him Class, but in public I called him by his new name: Derrick. Something was on his mind.

"Class, what's wrong, what did the agent say?"

In a sad voice, he answered. "My mom had a stroke. She's in a coma."

CHAPTER 9

<u>COREY</u>

<u>ATLANTA</u>

Federal penitentiary

"My name is Sherry Anderson. I want to thank you for granting *Streets is Watching* magazine an exclusive interview with you."

"Ya'll keep it real. Ya'll don't sugarcoat shit like other magazines tryna copy ya'll style. Plus, I know your man Ms. Anderson, real dude."

I'm surprised the warden and the bureau of prisons approved this visit. Maybe they're fishing for information for the government. You know how conniving the federal government is. I know Sherry isn't a government agent and she knows the limit to our conversation. I'm just shocked that they allowed this interview.

"Sitting in the visiting room by ourselves with one guard who never pays attention is tempting. Sherry is a bad chick. She smells good, looks good and dresses fly. She's all that. I can't help but to stare at her thick toned legs while she sits with them crossed. Her tan skirt is gripping her thighs like a latex glove making my dick hard as a brick. She looks like my favorite actress Sanaa Lathan minus the sexy scar Sanaa has on her jaw line.

"Can I call you "C" that's what you're known on the streets as, right?" Sherry asks in a sexy voice.

"No doubt."

Her smile lit up the room. She flipped her notepad open and I guess that was the signal for the interview to begin. "For the record, tell me where you're from."

"I'm from the Southside of Jamaica Queens, 40 projects to be exact," I answered with pride.

"I did interviews around the neighborhood. You and your crew are legends in the area," Sherry commented.

I'm not the type to toot my own horn, that's corny. I won't front it's definitely an ego booster to be labeled a legend in a legendary neighborhood.

"If that's what they say. Who am I to argue with them?" Sherry chuckled.

"I see you have a sense of humor too."

"You got to laugh in a position like mine to stop you from crying, feel me?"

Sherry's hand was moving fast as she wrote down my every word. They didn't allow her to bring a recorder in the prison, I'm sure that was nerve wrecking.

"They say you're being transferred out of Atlanta soon. You just got here, why the quick transfer?" Sherry asked with a serious look on her face.

"They say for security reasons. I have ties to Atlanta on the streets so they want me out of here.

"What dealings did you have in Atlanta?"

I paused before answering; I had to make sure I chose my words carefully.

XXXXXXXXXXXXXXXXXXX

<u>2002</u>

When Class brought me and Malik to the ATL the first thing he did was introduce us to a street legend he met in Lewisburg by the name of Geech. Geech was the head of a crew started in ATL called "The Street Mob." The street mobs' arms stretched up and down the east coast from

Florida to Boston. From what Class told me, Geech was an unusual type of gangsta. He moved to Atlanta to attend Clark University as an engineering major, winning him the moniker in Lewisburg "intelligent hoodlum." Born and raised on the streets of Pittsburgh, the six foot four solidly built, dark skinned giant with whiskey colored eyes and a short afro had a humble disposition. He is extremely articulate and soft spoken. When first meeting him you would think he's a college football player waiting for his chance to go pro. You would never guess that he was the ruthless head of one of the country's most dangerous drug gangs.

Geech paraded me, Class and Malik around the ATL, stopping off at it's many clubs, restaurants and what the city is famous for--strip clubs. Class told me Geech's re-up of cocaine on a monthly basis was somewhere between 300 and 400 bricks of the most potent cocaine in the country. Yet, he drove around in a gray Chrysler Sebring. He wore no jewelry, not even a watch and he wore Dickies a tee-shirt and a pair of scuffed up Timberland construction boots. To top it off, he worked as a counselor for a youth center in the Mechanicsville section of the city, funny dude.

It was at a strip club where I met this girl with a thick, big booty and small waist. She was a brown skinned, five foot three inch beauty. Geech introduced us to her, you would've thought he was making a cash deal for us to meet.

"I want ya'll to meet my wife and the owner of this club."

Her name is Stephanie, but everyone calls her Steph. She made sure me, Class and Malik got the V.I.P treatment at the strip club. The top chicks in the club gave us lap dances and "special treatment" in private rooms in the basement of the joint.

When Geech invited us to be guests at his home on the outskirts of the city, I finally saw how Geech spent his money. From the outside, the house looked like a plain upper class suburban, two story brick home in a quiet, well landscaped area. When we got inside, the marble foyer made held my breath. He had a fountain built in the foyer with Greek statues. Water flowed out of the statues penises, and a large crystal chandelier hung over the fountain. The house was straight out of MTV Cribs. There were security cameras all over the place. There were five bedrooms, three bathrooms, an Olympic size swimming pool in the back and a basketball court. In the basement, Stephanie had her own salon where she hired a few of the dancers at the strip club to do hair. In their two car garage Stephanie had a 2002 silver Mercedes Benz that cost a pretty penny. These two were living it up for real.

Geech had a connection in Florida that sold keys of coke for cheap. In fact, Geech was getting a key for fourteen five. In 2002, wow! Geech promised Class in Lewisburg that he would plug him in to the connect when he got out of jail after serving five years for a gun charge. Geech and Class had that in common.

Fortunately for me, Trish went into labor when we were in the ATL and Class rushed back to New York to watch the baby being born.

Geech, this is my brother. Go head and plug him in." Those words were music to my ears and if I had my way down in the ATL, Stephanie would be mine also. I got to find out how loyal she is to this big nigga first. Money talks, right?

Malik stayed in the ATL with me for two weeks. In those two weeks we stayed in a guest room in Geech's house that was the size of a project apartment. Out of respect, we didn't bring any girls in there to get crazy with, so we spent most of our time at different hotels doing all types of ménage trois, orgies with plenty of thick southern chicks all courtesy of Stephanie.

Geech introduced me to his Florida connect, a short, old Cuban guy who looked like a bullfighter with a big handle bar mustache and black hair that needed to be cut. He actually had a mushroom cut bang and all. He wore a thousand small gold chains around his neck, the Mr. T starter kit we call it. His 70's style butterfly collared shirt was open at the chest where the necklaces rested against gray chest hair. This dude wore the tightest slacks and cowboy boots, if he wasn't the connection, I would've taken him for a drunk Spanish guy who worked in a factory and spent his money on those gold chains and beer. Since it was my first time dealing with the Cuban, I copped fifteen keys from him. We drove down Atlanta's Peach Tree Street in his midnight blue Ferrari. He told me how he would send the stuff to New York.

"I own a charter bus company. I got a bunch of senior citizens going to Atlantic City this weekend. I'll put the stuff on the bus. The driver is one of my guys. You'll have to get it from him in Atlantic City." The Cuban said in a thick Spanish accent. This dude wore too much cheap cologne. He was killing me in the car. And oh yeah the Ferrari is special I got to cop one.

"No problem," I told him and it wasn't one at all. I would have somebody waiting in Atlantic City hours before the bus showed up. Geech spent most of his time doing the counseling thing while Stephanie and her girlfriends showed us around the town. Stephanie was 30 years old but looked like she was 20. I could tell she worked out in that home gym. Her stomach was ripped and her arms had definition. She was built like Melyssa Ford with the face of Nia Long. She was a flirt too.

"You got pretty hair," she said. When Geech wasn't around, she braided my hair placing my head between her thick thighs wearing a pair of spandex shorts. The pussy print looked like a small fist. Malik met a college chick and spent a few days rolling around in the sack with her, which gave me time alone with Stephanie. Either Geech trusted this woman or he didn't give a fuck about her. I couldn't tell. I know I wouldn't spend money like that on a chick I didn't give two fucks about. The second sign of Stephanie's interest in me was the day she confided in me about her husband.

"This nigga is never home. He spends all his time doing this counseling thing. We use to spend all day with each other. Geech used to be so romantic."

I listened attentively to her talking about walks on the beach, flowers and all that romantic bullshit they did together and felt it was my time to move.

"I would buy you the world everyday ma, I swear" I said tryna seduce her. I looked her in the eyes while I spoke. "If he don't realize he got a star on his hands, he never will."

Stephanie smiled. "Is that right?" she said. I couldn't read her body language or the expression on her face. Then I got more confused when she said. "I forgot I had to meet my girlfriend for lunch. I'll see you later." She just left. Before she returned, Malik and I were on a flight back to New York

Class picked me up from the airport in a brand new 2002 black Yukon Denali. When we got in the truck, Class had an angry look on his face. "For a nigga who just had a baby you look like you lost your best friend," I said reclining the passenger seat.

"Yo Cee, a bitch is going to be your down fall man," Class growled.

"Fuck is you talkin' bout?

"That nigga been with that chick Stephanie for years. Did you actually think she was going to give you the pussy?

You ain't got half the money dude got or history with her. She told the nigga you tried to come at her. He tests niggas with her."

I waved it off as if I didn't care. Really I didn't, but damn that is some gangsta shit she did. I knew something was strange about the bitch.

"Lucky ya'll got out of there when ya'll did. That nigga had a thousand niggas looking for ya'll. They weren't coming to fight.

Fuck Geech and that broad. Geech got guns, we got guns. Some of the coke I got from the Cuban I used to set up shop at this stripper's crib in the ATL. I put dope down there and got it poppin'.

XXXXXXXXXXXXXXXXX

"How do you feel about your co-defendant Nafiys Muhammad's verdict?" Sherry Anderson asked ready to write on her pad.

"That's a good thing, good for him. I don't wish this jail shit on my worst enemy, so if it's somebody I'm cool with, it's a beautiful thing."

Honestly I don't give a fuck about Nafiys. That nigga ain't gonna look back, he ain't do nothing for me, so fuck him. It's about me now. I never should've fucked with any of them dudes, my brother or Nafiys. I didn't need them. I made the Black Top Crew what it was. When my brother was on lockdown I made this thing big. I put him on top. Before he went to jail we were alright, but when he came back I was bigger than we've ever been. We didn't need Nafiys, he ain't really bring anything to the table that wasn't already there.

"We're doing a story that's pretty much part of the history of this crew. We're doing a thing on Bish Parker. We know your brother ran with him in Lewisburg. What do you know about Bish Parker besides him being your brother's girlfriend's uncle and one of Nafiys' and Class' mentors?"

Is she kidding me, I never met the old nigga. Obviously he ain't teach my brother shit or his niece, look what they turned out to be. I don't care about no old, dead nigga. If it ain't about me getting out of jail or about me, it's irrelevant. "Nah, I never met him."

"Ok Cee it's been nice meeting you and talking to you," Sherry said getting up from the red plastic chair. I couldn't help but to stare at that plump booty of hers looking like her butt cheeks were trying to escape from her skirt. Her dude is a real nigga and all, stand up dude. I met him on a few occasions at the gambling spots uptown and I bumped into him in Vegas. We weren't tight like that, just two hustlers who heard of each other and respected each other's rep. We weren't a team, so ain't no guilty feelings on my part tryna bag his lady.

"Ok Sherry. I hope I get to see you again, maybe without the magazine business." I hit her with that charming voice I come at broads with.

Sherry smiled before saying. "You read about me and my man, there's nothing coming between that." All I could do was watch her walk away with that sexy strut, can't say I didn't try.

Chapter 10

Malik

<u>Long Island Jewish Hospital</u>

I hate hospitals. I hate the smell, the whole vibe about them. What I hate more is sitting, watching my grandmother damn near dying from a stroke. Half of her body was paralyzed from it, strokes ain't a joke. I feel bad about this. Maybe me stressing my grandma out caused this stroke, added to the stress of Uncle Corey getting life and that rat ass Class helping them put Uncle Corey away. It all came too fast and too furious for grandma to handle.

I'm glad she's out of the coma and able to talk even though her speech is slow. Doctors say she will recover. It wasn't a stroke that completely destroyed her ability to recover, that was music to my ears. When she is able to get up and out of this hospital I'm going to take her on a vacation, probably to Hawaii or the Cayman Islands, get her away from New York for a minute. I need a vacation too. I've been busy running the crew I built after my uncles went to jail. Ya'll may think running a crew is easy when a lot of money is being made, but it's not. It's hard cash. You've got to trust dudes to watch the workers, make sure the product is on the streets and the money is right. You can't allow mistakes or anything short, so you've got to constantly go upside somebody's head. I have to put that all behind me for a second and take care of my grandmother.

TAP! TAP! TAP! The knocks on my grandmother's hospital door snapped me out of my thoughts. When the door opened I saw a pretty lady I never saw before. Damn she is sexy. "Hello this is Phylicia Classon's room right?

"Who's asking?" I said skeptically.

The lady walked toward me with her French manicured hand extended. "My name is Sherry Anderson. I'm from the *Streets Is Watching* magazine. Are you the nephew of Corey Classon?"

I read one of those magazines. It's a bunch of has-beens talking 'bout the old days and a bunch of dry snitching stories on what the government can do to catch you if you don't do this or that. The game is to be sold, not told. Gangsta's don't do magazine interviews. I heard my uncle did an interview before he got transferred to Leavenworth. I have to holla at him about that, he's losing his mind.

"Yeah I'm his nephew. And I'm not with the interview shit, so please leave." The smile on the lady's face immediately disappeared. "I'm sorry to bother you. I pray your grandmother gets better," she said then walked out.

From what I was told, my uncle told the magazine about our dealings in Atlanta. Atlanta was the shit. Yeah, we had the ATL poppin'. I've got to make my way back down there.

XXXXXXXXXXXXXXXXXXXX

2003 ATL

"The bitch got a man but he's lame. She said we can use her crib," I explained to Corey as we made our first trip to the ATL after the Geech incident. Corey knew Geech would be looking for him with his goons if he found out he was back in Atlanta. Corey didn't care; he brought his green army bulletproof vest, an AR15 and an AK with him.

We drove down there in a rented cream colored minivan. We boldly drove with the guns, a brick of dope and two bricks of coke to set up shop in some projects where this stripper I met lived. Her baby's father was a petty hustler who we planned to put to work so he wouldn't have beef with us moving shit out the crib. She told me he wasn't a gunslinger so he wasn't a threat.

When we finally got to see the dude, I couldn't understand what a pretty chic with a banging body like Tawanna was doing with this dirty ass clown. This nigga was a straight bum. He was a tall, lanky black nigga with short dreads, with fake football jersey's and knock off Evisu jeans. His whole wardrobe was knockoffs. I think Tawanna slipped up on a drunk night, gave the clown some pussy and got knocked up. She doesn't believe in abortions so she kept the baby. She was kind hearted and let the nigga stay at her crib so he could help her with the bills with his nickel and dime hustle. That's how I saw it, 'cause she gave me the pussy whenever I came to Atlanta. All she talked about was how her baby's father was in the way. If she wasn't a stripper and such a freak she could be wifey material. Tawanna is a dime, honey complexion, long silky hair, D cup titties, chink eyes, and a big round bottom topped off with a small waist straight out of the eye candy section of your favorite rap magazine.

Corey and I finally got to Tawanna's project apartment. She hooked it up like she didn't even live in the projects. There was a 60 inch plasma and wall to wall plush red carpet. Tawanna was what you called ghetto fabulous. She lived in Section 8 housing and made money stripping while collecting a welfare check every month. She definitely milked the system. Her 4 year old daughter is the direct resemblance of Tawanna, attitude and all. She walks around with her mother's stilettos on as if she were a model, eventually falling 'cause the shoes didn't fit. She was quick to stare you down, as if I needed permission to be with her mother. She would roll her big brown eyes at you if she didn't like you. To me she was adorable; I bought her candy every time I showed up, so she liked me.

Tawanna took one look at my Uncle Corey and her eyes almost popped out of her head. She knows I didn't sweat the fact that she was awestruck by my uncle. Our relationship was strictly physical. I wasn't there to get in her way and she wouldn't get in mine. She showed my uncle some "southern hospitality." She went from braiding his hair to trying all types of sexual positions with him within two hours of us being in her apartment. Tawanna is my age and she told me she likes older men like my uncle.

Tawanna introduced us to her baby's father when he came home from a night of petty hustling. When he walked in, my uncle and I were laid out on the sofa bed in the living room while Tawanna and her daughter were sound asleep in her room.

He tried to give me and Corey the murder one look when he turned the light on. "Ay what's up, shawty?" he asked with a gruff tone. He looked confused when my uncle and I looked at each other and bust out laughing. We were almost in tears.

"What, ya'll niggas high or something?" he grimaced.

"Yo, sit down my man, lets talk," Corey said with a serious face. The guy looked Corey up and down as if Corey were mistaken.

"Hey shawty, you got me fucked up."

Corey stood up and pulled out a chrome .45 automatic and cocked the hammer back. "I aint gonna say it again. Sit yo ass down. I'm tryna get you hip to something lil' nigga!" Corey stood in the guy's face. He was a little taller than Corey, but he seemed smaller once Corey approached. He sat down immediately.

My uncle told Teddy that he was going to help him make a lot of money. Teddy was all ears. You could tell the more he listened to Corey, the opportunity to make more than he ever did outweighed any fear or hatred he had for the New Yorkers who practically invaded his baby's mother's home. Within a few weeks Teddy turned out to be a good hustler. We spoon fed him an ounce of coke at a time; eventually we had to up his consignment. We didn't even know where he was selling the stuff. We just chilled at Tawanna's house all day playing PlayStation, smoking weed, sexing Tawanna's stripper friends and Tawanna. She didn't let me and my uncle hit it together, she would sex me one day and my uncle for the rest of the week. She was falling for my uncle and I guess giving me sympathy sex. I didn't care as long as she didn't. Tawanna really should have controlled her feelings for my uncle. I know my uncle and he was definitely into the business of breaking hearts. I got a feeling Teddy knew she was fucking one of us, but the money he was making with us detoured his attention away from her and whatever she was up to with the guys from "up north."

It wouldn't take long for Teddy's emotions to get the best of him when it came to us New York niggas. He had enough, especially after he snuck in the apartment one day and crept into Tawanna's room. She was giving Corey head that had his eyes closed and toes curling.

"Yo bitch, what the fuck you doing?" Teddy yelled. Tawanna jerked her head up so fast the cum she was about to swallow dripped down her lip. She almost choked on some of the hot liquid as she tried to mumble something that neither Teddy nor Corey could understand. Teddy turned his attention to a half naked Corey who was smiling as he got off the bed.

"Yo nigga, you ain't got no respect. Ya'll goin' do this while my daughter is sleeping!" Teddy pointed to his daughter lying on her stomach beside Tawanna.

"Take that up with yo bitch nigga, don't aim your anger at me. I'll break your fucking face," Corey threatened. Tawanna swallowed Corey's juices while covering her chest with her sheets.

"Teddy, Cee is my man now so you got to deal with it." Teddy stared at her menacingly then he looked at Corey and shook his head. He removed a wad of cash from his pocket and tossed it on the bed.

"Here's your bread homey. I'm out."

With Teddy out of the picture Corey and I had to recruit a new soldier who would move our stuff. We stayed in the ATL for two months straight. It was time for us to take a trip back up top, see family, regroup and come up with another plan for the ATL. Though we had Teddy off of our mind, Teddy had us on his. He had a plan, a plan that would turn things from bad to real bad in the ATL.

Chapter 11

<u>Sherry Anderson</u>

The worst part of my job is doing interviews with inmates. The hassle you have to go through to get inside of prison to visit someone is a serious headache. It's even more intense because my visits are considered high risk.

Interviewing infamous criminals or criminals in general for media purposes is high risk because authorities don't want criminals making comments about prison staff, security or the Federal Bureau of Prisons. We can't bring cameras or recording devices, so we're searched thoroughly. If it wasn't for the financial benefits that the magazine brings for me, my family and staff, I wouldn't be doing this.

Entering the visiting room of the women's Federal Correctional Institution in West Virginia, by the looks I received from the inmates you would have thought I just entered a male prison and became the object of their lust. What really caught me off-guard is when some of the women made cat calls and verbal advances even with loved ones and family members sitting with them. I ignored the coquettishness and proceeded to the table where my interviewee sat in an orange jumpsuit looking like a shell of her former self. Stephanie's hair was pulled back in a tight ponytail. She stood up as I approached the table. Her smile was bright, but forced. She looked a little older than 38. She wore no makeup, and her skin had deep craters. The pictures Stephanie sent me when we started corresponding were a lot different from her looks now. Stephanie subscribed to *Streets Is Watching* and she wrote a letter to me saying how much she loves the magazine. She loves the way we "keep it real" and how we "show both sides of the game, without sugarcoating it."

Before getting down to business we exchanged small talk. She complimented my hairstyle, my French manicure and how pretty I was. We spoke about prison life and how it affected her family.

"I miss my kids so much and I miss my husband," she grunted with teary eyes. I gave Stephanie time to compose herself before I said another word. Wiping tears from her eyes that had bags under them the size of almonds, Stephanie chuckled.

"I'm sorry, I just get real emotional when I talk about my kids and my husband's murder."

"Speaking of the murder of your husband. You know *Streets Is Watching* is doing a story on the Black Top Crew. This interview is part of that story. Class testified that his brother, Corey Classon was responsible for your husband's murder. Also a girl who used to dance at your club testified against Corey." I had to look at my notes to remember the girl's name. "Her name is Tawanna Catchings. I know you won't and can't tell us about the murder of your husband…"

"I aint never been nobody's snitch," Stephanie growled.

"I wouldn't want you to be that either. Can you tell me about this chick Tawanna and what you know about Corey Classon."

XXXXXXXXXXXXXXXXXXXX

<u>2003 Atlanta</u>

"Yeah baby, this nigga is a snake," Stephanie grumbled on her cell phone while cooking a pot of gumbo in the kitchen of she and Geech's home.

"I knew that from jump street baby. His brother is good peoples, I'll tell him about it. I got a plan for the nigga though. He's greedy, he'll be back in Atlanta," Geech responded. He smiled when he hung up his cell phone sitting in his cherry colored Ford Explorer he rented from Avis while he spent a weekend in Florida.

When Corey and Malik got back to Atlanta, Corey decided to visit Steph's strip club hoping he would run into her. He remembered hearing Tawanna on the phone with one of her friends talking about Steph and Geech breaking up. The mention of Geech and Steph put Corey on full alert. She didn't know that Corey was in the house while she did her toenails. At least Corey didn't think she knew he was there.

"She still runs the club, but Geech is out of the picture. They say he found out she was creeping on the low. I guess she don't need him no more. The bitch is paid," Tawanna gossiped.

Corey entered the club by himself dressed in a canary yellow linen short sleeve button down shirt opened at the chest revealing his diamond link necklace, a black pair of linen slacks with black Caesar Paccioti loafers. His 2 karat canary yellow diamond earring sparkled as the strobe light reflected off of it. Juvenile "Back Dat Ass Up" blasted as a naked brown skin voluptuous goddess did acrobatic moves on a pole while men and women threw money and compliments at the dancing beauty.

Corey sat at the bar smiling at females who flirted and glared at him. If he wasn't on a mission, he wouldn't hesitate to solicit a rendezvous with one of the under-dressed females, but he was focused. He was there for Steph. Not only did he want to sample her goodies, but he knew he could get super rich dealing with the business minded, hustling Stephanie.

From an upstairs office window, Stephanie spotted Corey sitting at the bar. She had to admit, the man was a cutie. She felt he was too old to have his hair braided, but she could look past that minor infraction. Stephanie decided to pay Corey a visit. First she sent him a bottle of Louis the thirteenth.

"The owner of this club sends you this," A half naked woman spoke to Corey and handed him the expensive bottle of liquor. Corey took the liquor smiling at her. She winked her eye at him and walked off shaking her tail feathers that looked like two midgets holding onto a string in between them.

"Don't stare too long you might get hypnotized," A voice whispered in Corey's ear, he knew it was Stephanie. He turned on the bar stool to face the sexy voice and face of Stephanie. Immediately, Corey undressed her with his eyes, removing a black spaghetti strap blouse and skin tight cream Apple Bottom jeans, but he left on the black 3 inch Blahniks.

"I wasn't staring, I was searching for someone," Corey replied.

"Did you find what you were looking for?" Stephanie asked with a smile.

"I hope so," Corey said flirtatiously. He held up the Louis bottle.

"Thanks for the bottle. I owe you one."

"How do you plan on paying me back?" She could tell he liked flirting.

"You name it," Corey shot back.

After the flirting, Stephanie asked what brought Corey to the club.

"I heard some things and I wanted to confirm them." Corey told Stephanie that he knew she told Geech that he came on to her. "I apologize for that. I couldn't help it. I mean it was hard to pass up on such a classy catch."

Stephanie blushed. "Self control is a sign of strength. Nothing is more of a turn on than a strong man, physically and mentally."

Her comment had Corey confused. Was she telling him he turned her off by coming at her or questioning his strength? Why was she flirting with him now?

"I accept your apology. You have to understand I am a loyal woman, by you coming at me when you knew I had a man, I felt you had no respect for me, like I fuck any cute man I meet," Stephanie said seriously.

"Nah ma, it was nothing like that. I just saw what I wanted and I went after it. I'm a go-getter, sweetheart," Corey explained.

Stephanie thought to herself. He's good, he really got his game down to a science, but he ain't as good as he thinks he is. "That's behind me now, just like Geech is. I'm a single woman now. So to pay me back for that drink you can take me to dinner."

I guess she's a go-getter too Corey thought. "No doubt ma, I got you."

Two nights later Corey took Stephanie to Justin's for dinner. Over plates of soul food they made small talk about each other's lives. Of course they were lying to each other.

"Geech listened to his sister who hated me since were kids. She spread some rumor that I was messing with this NBA nigga who comes to my club. All I do is make sure A-list customers get the V.I.P treatment and I socialize with them. You have to network in order to make other moves in life. It's not what you know, it's who you know."

"So where is Geech now?" Corey inquired.

"Back in Pittsburgh," Steph lied.

After dinner Corey took Stephanie to see a movie at the Magic Johnson theatre. While watching the movie Corey tried to slide his hand up Stephanie's dress. She held his hand back. "There's a time and place for everything."

She kissed Corey's lips softly while pulling her dress down. After the movie they drove around the city in his minivan.

"I know you're down here making money. Are you making what you're supposed to?" Corey was reclined in the passenger seat confused by her question.

"What am I suppose to make?" Corey asked.

Stephanie gave him an honest answer, the only true statement she made while spending time with Corey. "Geech and I moved here from Pittsburgh dead broke. Within a year we had a million dollars between both of us. I opened my club and Geech went to school and did his thing on the streets. The rest is history."

Corey lifted the seat up and looked Stephanie in the face.

"Show me the way Steph."

That's exactly what she did. She washed his money through her club and helped him open up a hair salon and barber shop in Bankhead. She provided him with mules (girls from her club) to transport heroine into Atlanta.

"Coke will get you money, but that boy-boy will have you drowning in paper." Stephanie told Corey.

Corey started making so much money that he forgot about one of the reasons he wanted to get with Stephanie, sex. Stephanie was happy that he forgot. She never planned on having sex with Corey, but she would've if Geech told her to in order to put their plan in motion. Then another problem came up that Stephanie had to get involved in: Teddy.

Tawanna did all the bagging up of heroine and coke in her project apartment. She gave out the product to workers and collected the money. Tawanna was probably one of the reasons Corey didn't stress about sex from Stephanie due to her willingness to do any and everything a woman could do to please a man sexually.

"Yo, she got that muscle control with her pussy, son. Her shit feel like her pussy is giving you head and pulling your shit deep in her," Corey told Malik one day while they were back in New York sitting in Malik's '03 burgundy Durango. Corey's phone rang.

"Yo!" he barked into the phone. Malik smoked his blunt while Corey listened to Tawanna yell on the phone. Malik could hear her rant.

"Calm down. I can barley hear you. He did what?" Corey grunted. Tawanna calmed down and spoke to Corey clearly. Malik watched as his uncle got that familiar look just before he did serious bodily harm to someone.

"Yo, I'm flying down tonight. Don't worry about him." Corey hung up his cell phone."

"What's the deal Cee?" Malik asked. Corey shook his head. "Tawanna's baby's pops robbed her and pistol whipped her."

"She ok?" Malik asked concerned.

Corey couldn't fly down to Atlanta with a gun, so he called Stephanie and told her to have some guns ready for him. Stephanie knew who Teddy was and told Corey. "I know who he is and where he stays. He's a dirty nigga. You don't have to do it yourself. I can get it taken care of."

"Na I wanna see his face before I remove it from his body," Corey shot back.

When Corey got to Atlanta, he went straight to Tawanna's apartment, something Stephanie told him not to do. Corey went to get his .45 he had stashed at Tawanna's. He knocked on the door with the secret code. Tawanna answered in tears. "Damn!" was all Corey could say when he saw her face. She looked like someone beat her face with a bat for hours. Her eyes were damn near shut and cheeks were swollen like she had tennis balls in her mouth.

"Why didn't you go to the hospital?" Corey asked hugging her.

"I was too scared to leave the house. Plus, the cops are going to ask questions."

"C'mon I'mma drop you off at the hospital. If they ask questions tell them you had a fight with a girl. That's it. Corey retrieved his .45 from under the sink inside a box of dishwashing powder. His placed it on his waist. Before they left he helped Tawanna get dressed and he cleaned her face with peroxide. Before they walked out of the house, Tawanna grabbed Corey's hand.

"Thank you Corey. I love you."

"Yeah I know c'mon we got to go." On the way to the hospital Tawanna stared at Corey as he drove attentively. A feeling of guilt overwhelmed her.

"Corey don't go after Teddy, That's what he wants you to do. It's a setup Corey, please don't go."

Corey ignored Tawanna, thinking to himself. Did she actually think I was going to let this nigga get away with taking my shit? I know he wants me to come after him. He had to know I was coming. Then, Tawanna dropped a bombshell. "Stephanie set this up Corey. They made me call you to tell you this. I wasn't gonna call you. I wanted nothing to do with this. Geech is waiting for you to go after Teddy, they plan on killing you."

Corey stared at Tawanna menacingly. He didn't say a word. He felt that Tawanna was telling the truth. She was a pawn in a plot that she had nothing to do with. She is powerless against the likes of Stephanie and Geech. Stephanie is good, real good. Corey dropped Tawanna off at the hospital. He thought about killing her, but changed his mind. Before Tawanna got out of Corey's rented Taurus she made one last plea.

"Corey, just leave Atlanta with me. Let's go to New York and be together. Don't go after them."

"Tawanna, get out of the car now!" Corey barked. Tawanna, in fear, did as she was told. Corey sped off, he went to Stephanie's club where she was waiting in her office.

As soon as Corey walked in, she handed him a blue steel .44 Magnum. "The nigga is in the house by himself right now, here's the address. He's in the back apartment so go through the front. I got the keys. My girlfriend lives in the house." Steph said. Corey just nodded his head and walked out of the office, I'll deal with Stephanie later. I got something special in mind for her, he thought.

The house was a run down rooming house on the east side of the city. Before Corey left the club parking lot, he checked the .44 Stephanie gave him. As he suspected the gun had blanks in it. He shot the gun at the car window and it didn't even break from the vibration of the loud bang. "Yeah this bitch is good."

Corey snuck through the back of the house after parking the Taurus two blocks away. The streets were empty at this late night hour. Everyone was out and about on the Atlanta night scene. Clubs, strip joints, parties and everything the black Mecca had to offer. Dressed in all black fatigues, Corey walked slowly through the small house after picking the lock on the wooden back door. The house was dark except for light coming from under one of the doors to a room. Corey heard the radio blasting. "Round Here" by Memphis Bleek, T. I. and Trick Daddy was playing. He heard voices mumbling inside the room. He put his head to the door.

"The nigga should be here in a few minutes. Steph just called and said he left the club with the blank pistol." Corey heard Geech say. Then he and Teddy started to laugh hysterically. "Dumb ass New York nigga."

Corey could tell they were looking out of a window when he heard Geech ask "you see a car coming? The nigga is in a green Taurus."

"Nah, not yet. Hold up, partna," Teddy mumbled. "Ok there the he go." Teddy snorted seeing the green Taurus pull up two houses down. They watched as a guy wearing a black hooded sweatshirt got out of the Taurus making his way to the house.

"This nigga think he real gangsta walking straight up to the crib" Geech whispered. "Hit the light."

Teddy cut the light off and Corey stepped back as both men crept out into the hall.

"It's your birthday niggas!" Corey snarled before he squeezed the trigger. Boom! Boom! Boom! The .45 slugs tore through Geech's back causing him to yell while a slug shattered his spine and the other two ripped through his lung and heart killing him. When the first shot rang out Teddy ran and made it out of the house. Corey didn't chase him, not wanting to draw attention to an already heated situation. The quiet neighborhood came alive as the echo of the gun shots interrupted the silence. The lights in other houses came on and shadows could be seen opening curtains to look out of the window. All that could be seen was a shadowy figure running up the street.

Teddy made it to his 1978 midnight blue Chevy SS and sped off. He dialed a number on his cell phone. When someone picked up Teddy panicked.

"Steph, shit is crazy. He killed Geech!"

Stephanie's heart dropped into her gator boots hearing the devastating news of Geech's demise. She didn't want to believe the love of her life was laying in some run down house bleeding to death from bullet wounds. Her life with him flashed in her mind. She couldn't imagine living without him. How could she go on? She asked herself. She regretted the whole set up of Corey. Why didn't they just ignore him? Why? Why? Why?

Stephanie snapped back to the situation at hand. She knew Corey would be coming for her. She quickly gathered up some of her things. She grabbed her nickel plated .357 snub nose out of her drawer, placed it in her Coach bag and headed out of the club. She told the bartender, a close friend of her and Geech for years they called Blue, to take care of the club for a few days. "I gotta head out of town for a few days. I'll call you." Steph rushed out the door and high tailed it to her 2 door cinnamon colored Lexus. She heard the screeching of tires before she opened the door to her car. She turned to see Corey's Taurus come to a halt and he jumped out of the car headed towards her. She removed the .357 from her Coach bag. Corey couldn't see her reaching for it. He didn't have his gun out and the last thing he thought would happen was Stephanie's next move.

Bam! Bam! Bam! Bam! Corey ducked and rolled under a car from the shots Stephanie fired at him. After the shots, he heard a car door slam and the sound of tires speeding off. He came from under the car, brushed himself off and mumbled. "That bitch is fo real."

XXXXXXXXXXXXXXXXXXXX

"So what exactly did you get arrested for?" I asked Stephanie after hearing the story of how she and Corey's lives clashed. I could tell it was extremely hard for her to speak of her husband's murder. She did well though, I must admit.

"They say I conspired to drug trafficking, murder and I laundered money for the Black Top Crew and my husband.

"How much time did you get?" I asked while writing down her answer.

"Life."

Chapter 12

<u>NAFIYS</u>

I didn't like the tone in Shabazz's voice. I'm hardly the type to be on the nervous vibe. I put an "H" on my chest and handle whatever comes my way; whatever Allah wills is supposed to happen. This time I can't front, when Shabazz interrupted my sleep with a call telling me to come to his office to discuss something extremely important. I knew that it was serious and I definitely wouldn't discuss it on the phone. Attorney client privilege means nothing to me or the feds.

"Baby girl, I have to go see Shabazz. I'll be back as soon as possible. You need anything?" I tapped a sleeping Ryan before I got off our king size canopy bed.
"No baby I'm good," she replied in a groggy voice, turning away from me, snatching almost all of the covers over her head. After jumping in the shower and putting on my frankincense scented oil. I put on a gray Akademik sweat suit and a white pair of Air Force Ones. In less than an hour I pulled up in Center City in my black on black Yukon Denali to my lawyer's office.

I entered Shabazz's spacious wall-to-wall carpeted office with all types of awards and certificates hanging on a wall along with a large rug with the Masjid in Mecca painted on it. Shabazz sat at his large oak wood desk looking as if someone in his family died. He stood as I approached, *"As-Salamu Alaykum,* Nafiys." Shabazz greeted me with a firm handshake.

"Wa Alaiykum Salaam," I responded.

I sat down in the chair in front of the desk and prepared myself mentally for what was bad news by the sound of Shabazz's voice and the look on his face.

"I'm going to give you the good news first," Shabazz began while placing his hands on the desk folded together. "I got a three month extension on your trial date." That was news I could use. I'm definitely in no rush to get back up in that courtroom for more drama.

Then, Shabazz took a deep breath and exhaled loudly before saying, "Your brother's murder was a setup." He paused. Hearing him speak of my brother's murder threw me off because I tried to put it behind me. My heart started pounding and my palms got sweaty.

"I know it was a set up. Why did you bring that up?" I asked curious as to why we were speaking about this in 2006.

"I found out who set him up for those J.B.M cats," Shabazz continued.

I sat up in the chair and stared him in the face. I could tell he was going to drop something heavy on my lap and I felt like I was getting in position to carry it.

"Lil' Butchie set him up for a guy named Chris that I represent. He just got locked up and is snitching his way out of it. He gave a statement to the cops a few weeks ago. I felt it only right that I tell you. I'm off his case because I can't represent both of you, but I had to let you know."

Yeah this was some heavy stuff, whoa! Blood boiling is an understatement for the way I'm feeling. Every negative emotion a human can feel is what I'm experiencing at this point. Niggas is wicked man. It's not even news that nigga is weak. He needs an army behind him to move. I know them dudes scared him into setting Bilal up.

"I know this is some heavy stuff to drop on you now right before your retrial, but I would've felt bad if I held this back," Shabazz said, interrupting my thoughts.

"Shabazz, you did the right thing. You did what a real dude would do for his friend. Loyalty is hard to come by in this game."

"I don't know what you're thinking or what your next move is. My advice is to let this case get by. Then do whatever you think is right.

Right or wrong isn't in the equation when it comes to this. What must be done is all that counts. Lil' Butchie is a jealous coward. He was jealous of my brother 'cause Big Butchie put my brother in a well deserved position over his son. Blood is thicker than water, but in the game, blood will make you bleed and the water will be what cleans the wound. Eventually the nigga would've tried to set me up. He has to be dealt with severely.

XXXXXXXXXXXXXXXXXXXXXXXXXXX

<u>South Philadelphia</u>

"The muthafucka is hiding out in Vegas under witness protection. My mother left his rat ass. The bitch is out there with him. She knows what time it is," Lil' Butchie said in a low tone half covering his mouth while he and his cousin talked. He was a short lanky dark skinned, short haircut thug called, "Beef" by his peers. (He earned the moniker one day in middle school. He was in a joking session with a couple of friends and a guy said that he resembled a "long piece of beef jerky." Everyone laughed hysterically and from that day on he was called Beef). They sat in Lil' Butches 05 H2 hummer on a dark street in the Tasker housing projects.

Lil' Butchie combed his beard that he let grow down to his chest. He let his beard and hair grow long to change his identity. He wore his hair in box braids that hung over his forehead. He didn't dress in his usual flashy style. He wore clothes that looked as if they were hand me downs.

"Yeah I spoke to her. She said she married the nigga under a fake name. She said he looked real different from the operation," Beef said while rolling up a blunt filled with potent angel dust. After rolling the blunt, he reached in his baggy Roca Wear jeans for his lighter. Lighting the blunt and taking a long drag holding the smoke in his lungs, he continued. "I'm heading down there tomorrow. I got a 9 o'clock flight. Everything is set up. Don't sweat it, I'mma handle my biz."

Butchie nodded his head. "Alright I'll be in New York for a while," Before Beef exited the Hummer he said.

"Butchie, for a nigga tryna lay low, a big ass Hummer is gonna draw, dog," Beef said before getting out of the Hummer.

Butchie shrugged his shoulders before pulling off. He dialed a number on his cell phone as he drove down the dark Philly streets.   When the person he was calling answered, he placed his phone on speaker so he could drive.

"Butchie wassup, where you at cause I gotta holla at you, you on some real bullshit" the female voice barked.

"What is it you're talkin' 'bout and watch your tone when you talk to me," he responded.

"The Internet Butchie, you put our tape on a fucking website. How could you do that? I'm out here in Vegas for yo ass and I look on the web and I see the tape we made that could fuck up the whole thing. You could get me killed you dumb ass!"

Butchie hung the phone up. "Does she know how many bitches I got on tape? She should feel lucky to have been with a dude like me."

Out in Vegas, Beef rented a car under a fictitious name and drove to a safe house that the woman who Butchie sent to Vegas to execute their plan rented also under a fictitious name.

When Beef got to the house, the woman was there sitting at a small wooden kitchen table with a large pair of 70's style shades and a dark, shiny wig that reached to the middle of her back with her shapely legs crossed. Her skirt was tight and above her knees showing the thickness of her thighs. She looked as if she just woke up from a long night of drinking. In fact she drank herself to sleep after seeing the sex tape she and Butchie made. She thought the tape was a private role play between her and the man she loved.

"What's up with you? You look like you got hit by the bottle," Beef commented. The woman lit a Newport cigarette and looked away from Beef.

"We're not here to talk about my life. Here's the address." She handed Beef a ripped piece of paper. "I left the door open, he'll be there tonight." The woman got up and left without looking at Beef. He watched as she walked out of the house. He couldn't help but to stare at her backside looking like it was going to tear out of the pistachio green skirt. "Damn!" Beef grunted after the door slammed.

Beef stayed in the small one story brick home, playing Xbox and smoking weed he brought from Philly until the Vegas sky became blood red from the setting sun. He performed the 4th prayer of the day of a Muslim before screwing a silencer onto a black 9 millimeter Ruger. Dressed in a black Dickie suit, he left the house and got in the black Dodge Neon he rented. When he got to the address, his mind was cluttered with so many thoughts. He was happy to have a chance to do this deed.

It was his time, time to erase the blemishes and wounds on the reputation of his family's legacy. He could feel the adrenaline rush through his body as he climbed the white picket fence in the backyard of the one story house.

Sweat dripped under his black Polo turtleneck from the humid, steamy Vegas night. When his feet hit the grass, he froze momentarily to look at the house and the one next to it. He glared at the windows of both homes waiting to see if any lights came on. Satisfied that he wasn't heard and able to silence the neighbor's dog with a prime rib he stuffed with a tranquilizer and tossed it over the gate; he proceeded towards the back of the home entering through a unlocked sliding glass door leading directly into the living room.

The alarm system was situated on a wall beside the glass door. The digital display said "system unarmed." Beef walked carefully through the dark home tiptoeing because he feared the black soft soul moccasins would make noise on the hardwood floor. He removed his gun from the waist of his Dickies and found his way to the master bedroom.

He knew the person he came for would be in a drug induced sleep from some sleeping pills the woman slipped in a drink she was supposed to prepare after a night out. She would leave the home with the excuse of visiting friends across town. Her only child was at a sleep over at one of her classmate's home, so he would have time alone at the house.

Beef pushed the white double doors to the bedroom open and immediately saw the print of a silhouette under thick gold colored Versace blankets. Beef smiled." I got you now you punk bitch."

The plush carpet made Beef feel like he was sinking. The canopy bed sat in the middle of the spacious bedroom with a white leather lounge chair beside it. Beef pointed the gun at the silhouette while pulling the blanket back. As he aimed the gun at the man's face, Beef stood in shock at what he saw. Anger replaced the shock at the sight of a contorted face with half of the head blown away, turning the gold satin pillow a dark burgundy. "Mother fucker!" Beef grumbled. He sat on the lounge chair holding his head in his hands.

"Who the...slimy bitch. She knew I..."

Beef stood up and pointed the gun at the mangled face. "Might as well get mine too." Beef pulled the trigger putting three bullets in the corpse's chest and made it jerk. Big Butch was dead as a door knob. "Can't fake this death, pussy!"

Beef walked out of the house the same way he entered. He quietly closed the sliding glass door and walked to the picket fence. Before he could climb the fence he heard a sound he dreaded, a sound every criminal dreaded. Things were about to get crazy.

"Freeze. F.B.I. Don't move! Put your hands up now!"

XXXXXXXXXXXXXXXXXXXXX

"I was told Li' Butchie hangs out in South Philly with his cousin," Shabazz tells me while looking at a file on his desk.

"I heard the same," I responded. If he knows what I know, he betta leave Philadelphia period. Philly ain't safe for Butchie anymore.

When I left Shabazz's office I had to drive around the city for a while to get my thoughts together. I had a lot on my mind, specifically Karma. What goes around comes around. I guess this is the beginning of nature and Allah's way of paying me back for all the wrong I've done. I never felt guilty about anything I did in the game. All the things I've done I felt were necessary for an evil lifestyle that I chose to live. I don't feel guilty about choices I thought deeply about and made. Shabazz's loyalty and good heart makes me feel guilty about one thing I've done, something I regret like hell.

Chapter 13

<u>Class</u>

The preparation for me to go to the hospital to see my mom was like the President was visiting a place and the Secret Service had to thoroughly check and sweep the place days before his arrival.

When I walked into the room filled with flowers that smothered the sterile hospital scent, I almost didn't recognize my mother. She looked much older than her 60 something years. Damn, I can't even remember my mother's age. Her hair was white as the bed sheets she laid on. Her face looked pasty and sunken. Her appearance sent a sharp pain through my heart. The guilt was killing me. I blamed myself for her stress that led to a stroke. I betrayed her and my family. I was also overwhelmed with fear, fear that she may not want to talk to me. Fear that she may become angry causing her frail heart to beat faster, probably causing a heart attack. I know she won't recognize me from my operation. It took a week for the visit to be approved by F.B.I. headquarters. I wasn't supposed to have any contact with family and old friends. I had to see my mother though, alive.

When I entered the room, she turned her head to look at me. I saw the confused look on her face, well the side of her face that wasn't paralyzed. "You got the wrong room, baby," My mother mumbled, her paralysis making her speech slurred.

"No I don't mommy," I said walking towards her with a bouquet of red roses. She stared at my face for what seemed to be an eternity. I could tell she tried to recognize the face that a familiar voice came out of.

"Jerry…Jerry is that you?"

"Yes mommy, it's me."

"Boy what these crackas did to yo face? Why you let them do that to you?"

My mother pressed the button to raise the head of the bed as I sat in a chair next to the bed. I still didn't get over the nervous jitters. I still didn't know if she would flip out on me after she got some words off her chest about the whole situation.

"Come here let me see your face." She put on her spectacles that had a beaded strap that she wrapped around her neck. I sat up and stood in front of her. With one hand, she held my face while turning it from left to right.

"These people are good." I could still hear her southern accent in her slur.

After she let my face go and removed her glasses, she leaned back on the bed. Her every move seemed like a struggle. She was apparently weak, I assume from medication, but she still had that fight in her. My mother is the strongest lady I know. She's seen it all in her life. She endured a lifetime of hardship and pain while keeping her spirits up along with her children and grandchildren. She is loyal to family. Family comes first after God. She looked at me and sighed. I could tell she had a lot on her mind. A lot she wanted to say to me. "Where are the baby and Trish?" she asked.

"At our new home in the Midwest" is all I could say. I wasn't allowed to give the exact location. It wasn't like my mother would send henchmen to our home, especially to hurt her granddaughter, but I don't know if the room was bugged and my mother could slip while she was on meds and tell someone else.

"How are they doing?"

"They are fine, Coco is in school doing fine and Trish is working as a hairstylist." I half told the truth. Coco was doing good in school but Trish...

XXXXXXXXXXXXXXXXXXX

Luckily for Trish, this thing with my mother's health came up 'cause I was definitely going to pick a bone with her. Sitting in my home office surfing through different websites and chat rooms, I came across a triple x site called Fantasy Fuck.com. It's a site where people sent in their own sex videos they made with wives, girlfriends lesbian lovers, and gay men. I viewed a few of the videos and came across one called "On Some New York Shit." I got the shock of my life. There in doggy style with her face directly in the camera was Trish with a dude who looked all too familiar pounding her back out. Turning the volume up Trish moaned and repeated his name. "Butchie beat this pussy up, oooh kill it kill it!" I almost hurled at the site.

At the time Trish was out of town, so I couldn't confront her about it. What would I say? What would I ask her?" She did what she did. There is no justification or explanation for this. There's' nothing she could say to make me excuse her for the acts. She had the nerve to be on a tape, though. She has no respect. The video was made before Coco was born so there is one question I need to ask. Was Coco mine? I didn't need Trish to be in town to find out. I took Coco to the F.B.I. office in Milwaukee and had the agent in charge get Coco and me a DNA test. The agent told me he would have the results in two days. The next day Trish came home and that's when I got the call about my mother's stroke. When I get back to Milwaukee I will get the results.

The whole week before I left for New York I tried to distance myself from Trish. I stayed in my home office for hours at a time while Trish cooked, cleaned and shopped downtown Milwaukee. The sex we had one time that week was routine. I performed in two positions, Missionary and doggy style. I ejaculated rolled over and went to sleep.

I decided to wait until the results of the DNA test to bring out the whole mess. Boy is it hard to hold all that in. My relationship with Coco hasn't changed. I love that girl. She is my daughter regardless. I raised her and she knows me as daddy, bottom line. If she isn't mine, Trish and I are done, and I'll fight for custody of Coco. I got the sex tape as evidence to show how unfit she is.

XXXXXXXXXXXXXXXXXXX

I was hoping my mom wouldn't ask me about my decision to rat on my brother and so-called friends. Though I had my reasons, how could you explain to your own mother about why you snitched on your brother? I guess she felt it was too late for questions.

"Jerry, there some things I have to tell you. Things I wanted to tell you all for years but didn't know how or see the reason I should speak on it." She spoke softly as if she were on the verge of revealing a deep, dark secret that was life changing. Her tone was also a tone of guilt. I stared at her attentively, looking into eyes that read and held a million stories. The crow's feet at the corner of her eyes seem to be growing as she spoke.

"Your father's name is Keenan Giles. He goes by the name of Tank, he's from Harlem." This was the first time in my life that my mother has mentioned my father. We grew up knowing nothing about the man, not even his name. My mother explained how they broke up after she found out he was a player in Harlem.

"At first, I ignored the rumors. I figured a lot of women in Harlem wanted Big Tank, the infamous friend and bodyguard of Ricky Barns." My mother said the words in a sarcastic tone." Big Tank, the infamous friend and body guard of Ricky Barns." I could tell those were names that left a bad taste in her mouth.

What shocked me is learning that my father ran with Ricky Barns, Bish did too. I wonder if Bish knew my father. He had to.

"Mommy, do you have any pictures of my father?"

"Oh, no. I erased everything about the man from my life. You and your sister and brother had his last name when you all were born. I had your last name changed to mine." I don't blame my mom for doing that especially after what she said next.

"The rumors ended when a woman showed up at my door with Tank's son in her hand."

"Son?" I barked. "You mean I have a brother somewhere out there?" My mother shook her head in the affirmative.

"And a sister," she continued adding more shock to the story.

"A sister too, how do you know about her?"

My mother told me of her friend Marquita from New Orleans who she met in Harlem and attended college with.

"When I moved us out of Harlem, Marquita stayed up there and told me about a girl Tank had by some lady from up there."

This is crazy stuff. Wow, I have a brother and sister I don't know about. I wonder who and where they are. Are they alive? Do they still live in New York?

"Where is my father, what happened to him?" I asked wanting to know all there is to know. My mother closed her eyes briefly while exhaling.

"I don't know where he is. He went to jail back in the day and testified against Nicky and a few of his friends. He should be out in the program you're in."

I know it was hard for my mother to tell me that, but I asked the question and she answered. It's like this snitching thing is genetic or something. My father is a rat too? Life is strange, ain't it? Oh shit! The thought came to me. Did my father snitch on Bish? Was he one of the guys Bish had crossed out in the pictures he showed me in Lewisburg? Nah, couldn't be that guy. Trish's father, oh double shit! My mother said my father had a daughter in Harlem. Trish is from Harlem. Nah, I know that aint it. Now that I remember Bish had more than one person crossed out in his pictures. I know one thing, when I get back to Milwaukee I have to do some investigating, some real heavy investigating.

XXXXXXXXXXXXXXXXXXXXX

Back in Milwaukee I headed straight to the F.B.I office to get the results of the D.N.A test. The agent in charge of my protection met me in the carpeted hallway with dull white painted walls and the smell of gallons of coffee filling the air.

"Mister Johnson, you're not the father of the child."

The news felt like the day I got arrested and indicted on RICO charges. How could Trish do this to me after all I've done for her? Why me? She got me raising another man's baby, that's probably why she didn't want operations for her and Coco. I guess she didn't plan on being with me forever, she knew all this time. Did she think I would treat her the way Corey did his baby's mother? She probably did. I'm not going to sit here and try to justify her actions. It's time to expose this no good bitch.

As soon as I got home, glad that Coco was still in school, I confronted Trish who was sitting at the kitchen table doing her nails while watching soap operas.

"Hey Class how is you're--"

I immediately grabbed the bitch by her ponytail and headed towards the office.

"Bitch don't 'hey, Class' me. You ho ass bitch!"

"Get off me, Class. What the fuck is your problem, what did I do!" Trish yelled frantically trying to escape my grip. I'm too strong for her though.

"Class, stop. Baby talk to me!"

"Oh we goin' talk alright. After I show you this, we're going to talk about how you getting out of this house."

When we got in the office, I turned on my computer and logged on to the website finding the sex video of her and Nafiys' homey from Philly. All the color left Trish's face.

"Class, let me talk."

"About what, Trish!" I yelled ready to choke the life out of her. I wasn't raised like that, though. I don't put my hands on women. I wouldn't let anyone do it to my mother or any women in my family, so I lived by what I preached.

I pulled a copy of the paternity test results from my sweat pants and threw it at a flinching Trish. "Read that. Coco ain't mine. Is she that dude on the tape's baby, huh?"

Tears formed in Trish's eyes and she put her head down in shame. She attempted to reach for my hand. "Class, listen, please."

I pulled my hand away. "Please what Trish? We are done!" I made an imaginary cut throat gesture with my hand. "Done!"

I don't know where Trish went, but she was gone for the whole day. She ran out of the house crying. I watched her jump in her '05 Galant and drive off. While she was gone, I decided to hit the computer and do some research on my family tree. After about a half hour of clicking the mouse from website to website, I came across a website that featured the story of Ricky Barns and a group of men in the organization known as "The Counselors."

XXXXXXXXXXXXXXXXXXX

<u>1979 Lewisburg Penitentiary</u>

"You honestly thought these guys were going to be loyal, it that what you really thought? A black suit and tie wearing federal agent growled in the lawyers visiting room at the Pennsylvania penitentiary. The tall, lean Roger Moore looking agent removed an 8 by 10 size photographs from a manila envelope and tossed them on the gray painted metal desk. Tank stared at the photos making different expressions on his face as he combed through the small stack.

Most of the pictures were of members of his crew standing in front of Harlem night clubs and bars, or exiting Cadillac's with various women in tow. Tank stared at one particular picture for a while. It was a picture of his close friend and confidant Bish groping Tank's girlfriend and mother of his daughter.

"These motherfuckers told me they were sister and brother," Tank snarled. The agent stood with one foot against the wall with his arms folded across his chest.

"Unless Bish is into incest that woman isn't his sister. No one cares, Tank. It's every man for himself in these streets," the agent said leaning closer to Tank's face.

Tank shook his head in disbelief. "What is it you want from me, why are you showing me this?"

"Well..." the agent started pacing the room. "You're a few years in on a very lengthy sentence. I can get you outta here way before the date that was set for you. Give me what I want and you'll get what you want."

"What makes you so sure you know what I want?" Tank asked.

"I never met a man who wanted to die behind bars," the agent replied with candor.

In a tone of defeat, Tank asked, "What do you want?" The agent smiled. "Gimme Bish Parker."

In 1979 Bish was serving time for possession of a controlled substance with intent to deliver at the Green Haven Correctional Facility in upstate New York. He was sentenced to 5 to 10 years. In 1979 Bish was a well built, athletic man with a fearsome reputation. He strolled the yard at Green Haven as if he were still commanding his crew on the gritty Harlem streets he once roamed. Bish was lucky enough to escape a major indictment that came down on his one time boss and confidant Ricky Barns. Bish got arrested in a separate case. One morning he was carrying a plastic shopping bag containing four ounces of dope to a bar so a bartender could sell it for him.

While Bish walked down Lenox that cloudy morning wearing a black turtle neck, gray slacks with a black pair of ostrich shoes, he saw a man trying to mug a young woman who lived on the corner of Bish's block. From across the street Bish yelled. "Hey blood, cut her loose!"

The mugger continued to try and snatched the purse out of the lady's hands. She held on for dear life screaming for someone to help her. The streets were occupied by dope fiends rushing to get their morning fix, so no one had time to intervene in a mugging. The mugger was probably dope sick and trying to get some money to rid himself of the pain caused by the physical need to have the dope.

Realizing that the mugger wouldn't stop, Bish ran over and started to punch the mugger on the side of his unkempt Afro styled head. The mugger was so eager to get money for his fix, he still didn't let go of the bag. Bish placed the bag he had in his hand on the ground and retrieved his holstered knife. He cut the strap of the bag, beating the mugger mercilessly. Bish or the mugger didn't notice a cop car pull up. Two cops jumped out of the marked vehicle and proceeded to separate the two men. The mugger ran off while the cops held Bish by his arms.

"Hey man, he tried to mug a lady and I helped her. You see he dropped the pocket book strap," Bish pointed to the strap left by the mugger.

"Ok buddy, that sounds good. Tell me this. What's in that bag you got there? Don't say it ain't yours. I saw you with it a few minutes ago when you came out of that building on 134th street."

"That's none of your business," Bish growled.

"Take his ass in. We'll see what's in the bag when we get to the station."

Bish wished he could've taken his words back. He was angry about the way the racist officers were talking to him. His adrenaline was pumping from the altercation with the mugger and he knew they would look in the bag anyway and take him in for it. On the drive to the precinct, Bish looked out at the bleak, zombie filled streets of Harlem knowing it would be a little while before he graced them with his presence. What he didn't know was that his 5 to 10 in the state system would turn into a life sentence in the Federal Bureau of Prisons with the help of his fellow comrades.

"Parker, they want you up in receiving," a correctional officer in Green Haven told Bish as he entered his cell block returning from lifting weights in the yard. His tank top was drenched in sweat and his brown skin glowed.

"What they want me for?" Bish asked curiously.

The overweight red curly headed hillbilly officer shrugged his shoulder sitting at his desk reading a hunting magazine.

"I was just told to send you up there," the officer said.

Bish went to his small cell and bird bathed before putting on his state issued green shirt and pants exiting the loud cell block heading toward the area where new inmates to the prison are brought in.   When Bish entered the receiving area, he was greeted by two men in dark colored cheap suits.

"Bish Parker?"   One of the agents spoke to him in a deep voice.

Bish looked at the man confused and skeptical. He also looked at a correctional officer who sat at the reception desk with a stack of paper inside a beige folder with Bish's name written on it.   The officer who was a captain at the prison, shrugged his shoulders as if he didn't have an idea of why these suited men wanted to see Bish.

"Yeah that's me," Bish replied.

The men flashed their gold badges displaying F.B.I emblems. "F.B.I. We're placing you under arrest and into the custody of the federal government of the United States of America."

All Bish could do was bow his head and sigh as the agents cuffed him and walked out.   They put him in the backseat of an unmarked Chevrolet Caprice and drove the few hours into the Metropolitan Correctional Center in Manhattan.   Bish was processed and booked, read his Miranda rights and informed of the charges.

"Mister Parker, you're being charged by the federal government under the R.I.C.O statue," the U.S. attorney for the Southern district of New York explained.

Bish heard the rumors on the streets about Tank snitching. He remembered receiving a letter from Trish asking if the rumors were true. He didn't have proof, so he said they weren't true. Now, he knew. In November 1979

Bish stood trial on the R.I.C.O charges. The day before trial he held a conversation on the phone with Trish's mother."

"Whatever you do, don't bring Trish to the trial. I don't want her to see Tee. This could have long effects on her seeing her father help bring me down."

"Ok honey, I love you."

Bish hung up the phone and sat in his cell pondering over the whole ordeal. Why? The question constantly ran through his head. Why would cats who swore to the code of the game break the code as if it never existed? Why do these cats act as if they're committed to the life, instead of letting it be known from the gate that they're not cut out for that part of the game? No one can tell me that they don't know they're not cut out until the pressure is on. The pressure is always on. Everyone who plays the game knows that a bullet or bars are waiting around the corner.

XXXXXXXXXXXXXXXXXXXX

Three nights after Class confronted Trish about the sex tape and the paternity of Coco, he tucked her in bed for the third night having to have to lie when Coco asked, "daddy when is mommy coming home?"

"Mommy called and said she would be back in two more days. She is going to bring you some nice toys. Don't worry lil' lady." Class kissed Coco on the forehead before leaving her room. As he walked towards the door, Coco whispered,

"Daddy, I love you!"

"I love you too." Since he found out that Coco wasn't his biological daughter, he secretly cried at night. He loved that little girl. To make matters worse, he had to remind himself not to change his attitude towards Coco. This wasn't her fault, and to think he became a rat to be with his family.

XXXXXXXXXXXXXXXXXX

What was I thinking? I asked myself. All this witness protection for what? I risked my life out on those streets to make this bitch's life glamorous. Damn, I'm a sucker. Well, it's another price to pay in this unforgiving thing we call life.

Chapter 14

<u>Rudolph Giuseppe Esquire</u>

<u>Ossining, New York</u>

Being the former U. S. attorney for the Southern district of New York in the 70's and 80's and the mayor of the country's largest city, I had one hell of a career with a lot of stories to tell. A lot of people during my tenure as mayor say I drastically changed the city's vibe. The conservative right wing says I changed it for the good and brought morale into a city with a history of hatred and crime. Liberals say I took away a lot of freedom of expression such as peepshows and strip clubs on the infamous 42nd street. Hell with the liberals. I did a lot of interviews during my political career, *Time Magazine*, *The New Yorker*, etcetera. This interview with Ms. Sherry Anderson from *Streets Is Watching* magazine I feel is a much needed one. I say that because one misconception about me and a lot of politicians is that we don't care about minorities and the poor people who live in the inner city. This interview is my opportunity to clear up that misconception and also an avenue for me to reach inner city youth and show them how a life of crime doesn't pay off in the long run.

"It's kind of odd that I live a block away from Sing-Sing, a place I sent a lot of criminals to," I said to Ms. Anderson as we walked down my tree lined well manicured lawn. The sunny afternoon was convenient for the walk and a quick stop at a coffee shop for some mocha lattes.

"I could never get used to hearing the alarm go off at the prison. Every time I hear it, I think one of the prisoners escaped and is headed straight to my home," I joked.

"What would you say to those people who say you're a racist?" Sherry asked me.

"I'm an Italian American and I've prosecuted and sent more Italian Americans to prison than any other group of people. So, do I hate Italians? Of course not, I love Italian culture. I was raised by hard working Italian immigrants who instilled hard working, positive values in me. My father worked the Brooklyn docks for years earning an honest buck to feed his family. It was a bad bunch of Italians who tried to extort and make life hard for honest Italians. There are bad apples in every bunch and those are the people I'm against. There are good people in every ethnic, class or group of people. I never showed favor to any particular group.

"Your honor," I blushed and was flattered by Ms. Anderson's use of the phrase. I haven't heard it in a while.

"You can call me Rudy."

"Thank you. You can call me Sherry, as I was saying, Rudy." Sherry and I chuckled at the first name relationship we established.

"I'm doing a story on a man named Keenan Giles, also known as Tank. He was part of the Barns organization, a case you prosecuted. What can you tell me about Giles?"

"Ah, I remember Giles well. Big guy, part of what they called "The Counselors" in Harlem. It was one of those cases that helped boost my career as a U.S. attorney. What a lot of people didn't know was that Giles had a lot of persuasive abilities. He was like a Mafia family's consigliore. He also was a real lady's man. If I remember correctly, it was a woman who caused him and his boss to cooperate with the government."

<u>1969, The Lenox Lounge</u>

The seven men dressed in tuxedos adorned with diamond cuff links, stood next to each other posing for a picture that they were about to take celebrating their success while most Harlem residents lived in a post-riot, dilapidated, war torn looking neighborhood in utter poverty. These men were responsible for the thousands of people in Harlem's daily fix of a potent Turkish heroine that turned the area into a grave yard of the living dead.

You would think people in the community would view these men as a plague destroying the fabric of Harlem, but when you live in a society that ignores the cries of the disenfranchised and offers no alternative to poverty, these self-made millionaires become their heroes. Those men offer hope to an ailing population. Soup kitchens sprang up on every corner, slum lords are put in check by these local legends. Amusement park trips and events for the kids are sponsored by these gangsters, motivating the normal citizen to turn a blind eye to the crimes committed by these hoodlums. Can you blame a single parent struggling to put food on the table for her kids for ignoring the illegal activities, when these hoodlums are the ones she can turn to when her lights are cut off and she can barely pay rent?

"Sharon, hurry up with that camera, girl. The food is getting cold," Big Tank growled at his woman who was preparing to snap shot the seven men. Friday nights at the Lenox Lounge always turned out to be a who's who in the Harlem underworld. Hustlers of all kinds congregated at the lounge to enjoy live music by artists like James Brown and other stars that frequented the Harlem night scene.

"Ok, smile for me!" Sharon a voluptuous golden brown beauty commanded before the light flashed on the camera. After the picture was taken, the men returned to the business of making deals with local con-men, stick-up artists, drug pushers and politicians. Political connections as high as the U. S. Senate, sometimes, broke bread with these hoodlums. Palms were greased at places like the Lenox lounge. Cops were paid off to let things run smoothly for these street entrepreneurs.

Some of the men dined with their girlfriends, wives and mistresses. Well, wives were rarely seen at the lounge, only on a few occasions and that was if the wife was somehow involved in the underworld. Men were usually accompanied by a girlfriend decked out in fur coats and expensive diamond jewelry.

Sharon was the girlfriend of Tank and a part of the Barns organization. She recruited women off the Harlem streets to work at Barns' spots where his dope was packaged. The women had to package the dope while they were naked. Sharon knew that Tank fooled around with a lot of women in a lot of different places. In fact, she knew Tank had a son by another woman in Harlem. She heard rumors that he had other kids around the city, but she definitely knew about the son who had Tank's name.

It didn't bother Sharon because she had a skeleton in the closet herself. As Tank mingled with his partners in the Lenox lounge, Sharon caught her handsome skeleton sneaking peeks at her. Her skeleton couldn't help but watch her as she worked the lounge wearing a red silk dinner gown that hugged her figure. Her perfectly round afro glowed under the dimmed lights along with her 1 karat diamond choker. Sharon also admired her skeleton's appearance. He looked sharp all the time. But this particular night he looked immaculately handsome in his tuxedo with a red bowtie that matched his red snake skinned shoes. His black fedora had a red band around it that also matched the tie and shoes. His sharply lined up side burns looked as if they were pointing at his dimpled cheeks that resembled the color of polished pennies.

"Why are you sitting here all by yourself Bish?" Sharon asked while standing in front of the table.

Bish removed the toothpick from the corner of his mouth. "I'm just enjoying the scenery. Soaking it all in."

"I brought you a--" the sound of gun shots erupting in the lounge jolted everyone out of their mingling and caused the crowded lounge to turn into a stampede. Pow! Pow! Pow!

Bish ducked and crawled towards Sharon who was already on the floor. He grabbed her by the hand. "Stay low Sharon!" he mumbled. Bish looked up to see where the gunshots were coming from. He saw two men at the entrance shooting towards Tank and a guy everyone in Harlem knew as "Guy". Bish knew he had to get out of the lounge. He knew the guys shooting came for the whole crew. There were probably more of them outside waiting.

Bish saw Tank crawling on his stomach holding the back of his leg. Tank was shot. Guy was under a table shooting back at the enemy.

"We gotta head out the back Sharon," Bish said reaching in his jacket for his.32 revolver.

"When I start shooting, run," he commanded Sharon who lay on the cold floor shaking.

"Run!" Bish barked. Sharon ran in a ducking position to the back exit of the lounge while Bish aimed his pistol towards the two shooters.

Boc! Boc! Boc! Boc! Bish ran backwards shooting at the same time. When he got out of the lounge, he saw Sharon hiding behind his black Seville.

"Come on, baby, get in!" Bish grumbled as he opened his driver side door and opened up the passenger door for Sharon. They sped off through the drizzling rain headed for Bish's Mount Vernon condo. No one but Bish knew about the place. When he wanted to get away from the hustle and bustle of the city and gather his thoughts, he would escape to his condo. Sharon was the first person he brought there. They rode the 30 minute ride from Harlem to Mount Vernon in silence. Sharon was recovering from the shock of the whole night and Bish was thinking of his next move. At the condo, Bish broke the silence.

"They shot Tee; I got to make some calls." He grabbed the phone off a coffee table and started dialing a number. Sharon stopped Bish's hand from continuing to dial.

"Sharon, what are you doing?" Bish looked at her confused.

"Tee's probably at a hospital. You ain't goin' find out nothing now that you can't find out tomorrow. Let's put this night behind us and wind down," Sharon said. Bish hung the phone up and leaned back on the black quilted sofa. Sharon walked over to Bish's small bar situated in the corner of his plush carpeted living room. The only light in the living room was from a large fish tank on the side of the bar. Sharon turned the light on as she walked to the bar. Bish removed his jacket and bowtie while placing an Al Green record in an 8-track player. As Al Green's voice filled the house, Sharon made her way to the couch handing Bish a glass of wine and sitting next to him. Bish let the wine fill his throat waiting for the effect of the alcohol to takeover.

"We've made a lot of people angry with the girl we've been moving. I recognized one of the shooters. They're from an outfit out of South Bronx."

"They got some mean cats up there. I guess this is just the beginning, huh?" Sharon inquired with a worried tone.

"You never know," Bish answered.

Sharon put her drink down on the glass coffee table in front of the couch.

"I wanna fix you something to eat but…" Sharon started to unfasten Bish's pants. "I'll have an appetizer before the main course." She pulled his semi-erect organ out and wrapped her warm sensuous full lips around him. Bish leaned his head back as her warm mouth made him fully erect. Sharon performed like a pro as Bish held the back of her head. Sharon pulled his pants down as she positioned her body in between his legs. With a free hand, she fondled Bish's testicles while still pleasing him orally.

The fondling caused Bish to moan and his toes to curl. Sharon stood up in front of him and lifted her dinner dress revealing her lingerie and thick thighs. She removed her white satin panties and straddled Bish. He palmed her plump rear end and squeezed as she rode him.

"Yeah baby. Ooh yeah, give it to me!" Sharon grunted. Bish granted Sharon her wishes. He leaned her over the back of the couch and entered her doggy style with his shirt and bowtie still on. Sharon felt Bish's love muscle deep inside her wet canal as it touched every space.

"Oh yes, fuck me!" Sharon panted. Bish looked down at his stiffness and watched it become soaked in Sharon juices. He pumped harder while palming her soft ass. The warm tight feeling of her cave made him grit his teeth. When he first started sneaking around Tank's back, having covert sexual rendezvous with Sharon, he felt a tinge of guilt, and he told himself he wouldn't do it again. He rationalized the affair with the fact that both of them were drunk one night, especially her.

They were both leaving a bar on Fredrick Douglas Boulevard and Bish offered her a ride home because she was a little too tipsy. It was one of his fellow Counselors' member's girls. The last thing on Bish's mind was violating the rules set up by the Counselors. One of the main rules besides not snitching was not sleeping with your fellow Counselors member's girlfriends, or wives. Bish wanted to make sure she got home safely. A rapist or mugger would take advantage of a woman staggering through the streets in the middle of the night alone.

Bish, when are you going to get a woman, settle down and have a family?" Sharon slurred.

Bish looked over at her and shrugged his shoulders. Out of nowhere, Sharon began to kiss Bish on the mouth. He pulled back initially, but Sharon's persistence won him over. A kiss ended up with him in her Brownstone, on her queen size waterbed going at it for two hours. Bish was hooked.

Bish exploded inside of Sharon as she climaxed for the eighth time during their couch love making. As they lay on the couch, Sharon rested her head on Bish's chest,

"Bish, I love you."

"I love you too, baby."

Sharon rubbed Bish's stomach and continued. "I have something to tell you."

"Talk to me, baby," he said in a comforting tone.

"I'm pregnant," Sharon said after a brief pause.

Bish sighed. "Whose baby is it?" Tears begin to well up in Sharon's eyes as she answered. It's Tank's."

Bish leaned up to face Sharon. He wiped her tears with his hands. "How do you know its Tank's?"

"It was before me and you first made love."

A year later, Sharon gave birth to a baby girl she named Trisha. That same year Tank got busted for murder. He didn't show up at his daughter's birth and he didn't sign the birth certificate. In fact, when Sharon told him she was pregnant, he didn't seem enthused about it. He began to distance himself from her. Bish spent more time with Sharon and her daughter than Tank. When Tank got locked up for murder, retaliation for the shootout in the Lenox

Lounge, Bish pretty much adopted Trish as his own. To save face with his crew, he played the role of an uncle who was holding things down for his fallen comrade. Secretly, Sharon gave Trisha Bish's last name.

Tank was always under the impression that Sharon and Bish were brother and sister from different mothers, but the same father. The truth was, Sharon's mother married Bish's father back in the 50's and they got divorced a year later. It was Bish who introduced Tank to Sharon.

In 1972 the federal government indicted Tank on a charge of interstate drug trafficking. He was taken to Rikers Island before his trial for murder and transferred to a federal detention center in Fairton, New Jersey. The feds found a car registered to Tank in Newark with five kilos of heroine in it. They tricked Tank into admitting the car was his.

An agent came to visit Tank on the island. "They say you used a Chevy Impala when you murdered that guy. I think that's a lie. They did find a Chevy Impala but you own a Buick, don't you?" The agent showed Tank a picture of the duce and a quarter." Is this black Buick yours? Tank, thinking he would be cleared of the murder immediately replied.

"Yeah that's my car. I never owned a Chevy Impala."

"Are you willing to sign a statement verifying that that is your car and that you had it parked outside of a Newark airport?" the agent asked.

"Hell yeah, I had it at long term parking first then I moved it," Tank answered enthusiastically.

"Can you give us the license plate number?" The agent asked.

"It's easy to remember. It said Tee's bird. That's what I called my car."

After Tank signed a statement and signed his name on the photograph of the car, the agents left. Two days later

Tank was transferred to Fairton and held there until his trial in 1973

XXXXXXXXXXXXXXXXXXXXXX

"When did Tank decide to turn on his crew?" Sherry asked me after recording things I said on a small recording device. We walked through a small park after our stop at a coffee shop. Sherry watched as I fed a bunch of pigeons a bagel I bought at the shop.

"Two years after he was convicted of drug trafficking and murder he called my office and said he had some info for me that could be of great value. I knew he had that type of information too, for the simple fact that we were investigating the organization and its connection to a Cosa Nostra family in the city. Tank was a high ranking member of the Barns organization, so I immediately took a personal trip to Lewisburg where they had him at the time."

"So, in 1976 Giles began cooperation with the government?" Sherry asked with her recording device close to her lips. I nodded in the affirmative.

"When was Bish Parker indicted for the crimes Giles talked about?"

"We investigated Giles' testimony and in 1978 Parker was indicted."

Sherry nodded her head and made a facial expression that showed she was in deep thought on another question she wanted to ask.

"Before we conclude this interview I have one more question for you your...I mean Rudy." Sherry chuckled at her mistake while I smiled.

"Is Giles in witness protection?"

"He used to be in, I think. In 1989 Giles refused witness protection telling the U.S Marshals that he doesn't want to live in fear until he dies. He also said he has no reason to hide from a bunch of dudes he considered cowardly snakes."

"So, where does a guy like Giles run to if people do start hunting for him?" I really didn't understand Sherry's question. Where else does a citizen of this country go when there is danger?

"The authorities, I hope. If I understand your question correctly you mean guys of his status. People like Giles still feel that using violence is the way to solve problems. If he takes that direction, he'll have the authorities in Arizona to answer to."

Sherry smiled real big with the answer to that question. Maybe she was elated that the interview was coming to an end and she got the story she was looking for.

"Rudy, it was an honor speaking with you. I know people in government and the authorities frown upon our magazine. They feel we promote crime, but that is far from true. We open people's eyes to what's happening in our urban communities and we don't water it down. We're making people aware of the consequences of living a criminal life. We do not glorify crime."

"You're welcome, Sherry. I feel honored that you all reached out to me so I can clear up some misconceptions about my political views."

I walked Sherry to her black '06 Mercedes Benz SLK55. I shook her small, soft hands.

"Nice car," I commented as she got in it.

She smiled back. "The best money can buy."

Chapter 15

Beef

<u>Vegas Office of the F.B.I</u>

"I'm going to ask you one more time… who were you with? We know you didn't act alone." Damn, this dude's breath is cranking. He thinks yelling in my face while I'm cuffed to this chair playing the bad cop role is going to intimidate me.

I really got him pissed off when I looked into the camera they had pointed towards me in the corner of the room.

"I didn't graduate from Quantico. I graduated the streets of South Philly. It's not my job to find out things, it's yours." I could tell that really pissed the agent off. His white face turned hot pink at my sarcastic answer.

"Listen, some of the bullets in the body matched your gun, so we got you dead in the wrong. You're gonna be in jail forever. You can save yourself by telling us who sent you."

I wish all my bullets would have been the ones that killed that rat uncle of mines. I wanted to look in his face before pulling the trigger how could he betray his family like that. Why would he try and set Nafiys up getting Lil' Butchie caught in the midst. He deserved to die.

"I sent myself. Can I make a phone call?"

After I was booked and finger printed, they sent me to the Clark County jail. The county jail wasn't as bad as joints like C.F.C.F. or P.I.C.C. in Philly. Clark County was kind of calm and laid back. The only violence was between a few gang members. Vegas had a lot of gangs, but the violence was nothing but a couple of scuffles.

I tried to call Lil' Butchie that first night, but all I got was his voice mail. I left a message for him to send me some money for a lawyer and for some commissary. I knew Butchie wouldn't turn his back on me. A good lawyer could at least get me a good plea bargain. They definitely got me. Somebody had to set me up though. It's like they were waiting right there for me, that no good bitch of Butchie's probably did that. I don't know why that nigga fucked with that bitch anyway. What's really crazy is that he married her. The marriage doesn't make sense, though. He shit on her like crazy. He fucks all different type of broads, tapes it and puts them on the internet and still deals with her. How could you trust a chick like that?

I left a message with my mom to get with Butchie and let him know the situation.

"What did you get yourself into out there in Vegas?" My mom cried.

"Ma, I can't talk about it on the phone. Just tell Butchie I need to hear from him a.s.a.p."

"Ok baby. I'll send you some money for cosmetics. I don't have that kind of money for no lawyer. My check ain't get here yet."

I definitely wasn't in a mood to hear a sermon from my mom. I needed a lawyer and fast. My mom sent me $50 dollars. I was able to buy cosmetics and some snacks. The food in the jail was alright. They didn't starve you like the county jail back home. There was definitely a shortage of food on state road.

A week went by and I heard nothing from Lil' Butchie. A week turned into a month. I went to a preliminary hearing and was bound over for trial on a first degree murder charge and conspiracy to commit murder. The conspiracy charge came from the theory that I and another person killed Big Butchie. My court appointed lawyer, a public defender who had no real homicide experience, two cases of murder that he lost, well, one he plea bargained, told me the conspiracy charge is definitely beatable.

"If they were tipped off about you going to the house to kill the guy and were waiting for you, why didn't they see the other person? Why didn't their informant tell them about the other person?" The public defender made a good point.

I'm not worried about beating the conspiracy charge. The charge won't stick, but why isn't this nigga Butchie playing his part. My mother told me she hasn't heard form him or seen him around South Philly. Then 3 months later my mother tells me he called.

"I spoke to Butchie; he said you were stupid enough to get yourself in trouble now get yourself out of it."

That was a blow that knocked the air out of me. "Hold up, ma. Lil' Butchie, your nephew said that?" I asked unsure of what I heard.

"Baby. believe me, I told that boy he wrong for what he saying. He just don't care. I told you 'bout running those damn streets thinking that these niggas care bout you. You can't even trust family."

My mother words faded out to me. All I could think of was my cousin. The dude that sent me on this mission, a mission to kill his own pops, my uncle because of his snake shit. He turns around and pulls this. Niggas ain't shit! You know what? I got something for his ass. That bitch don't know who he fucking with. He done fucked up for real! He don't even dig it. I got this card right here, let me use this phone. All the noise from the rest of the inmate's playing cards and watching T.V will give me a little privacy. No one will hear this conversation.

"Yeah hello, can I speak to Agent Rowland." A female secretary put me on hold. This nigga Butchie goin' pay for this shit. "Yeah Agent Roland this is Maurice. I got to talk to you about something."

Chapter 16

Lil' Butchie

Fairmont Park, Philadelphia

There is nothing like a morning jog to relieve stress. The fog makes the air thick and difficult to run in, but I'm in shape so I can handle it. I wonder how things went in Vegas. I should be getting a call this morning letting me know. Twelve miles is good enough this morning (Butchie waves his hand at a black Lincoln Town car driving slowly behind him.)

Once in the back of the Lincoln, I removed the hood of my Polo sweat suit from my head. I wish my phone would've rang after I caught my breath, but I know its Vegas so business has to be tended to.

"As-Salaamu Alaikyum. You got some news I can use?" I asked after greeting my caller. I didn't want to be on the phone long. My caller gave me the answer I was waiting anxiously for. "The cheese is off the rat trap." Then hung up.

I can't stop myself from smiling. I'm feeling the whole situation. My father has been betrayed me since he put Bilal in front of me, his own son. Then he tries to set Nafiys up through me on some police shit. He didn't care if I got killed or not. I'm glad my mother left his ass. My mother respects the code. I can't tell her what I did, but I don't think she would care. She was under the impression that he died from a heart attack. This time the feds help him fake his death so he could hide. Not this time.

"Driver, go to New York so I can pick my wife up."

About an hour into the drive, something told me to check my voicemail. I didn't check it in a while. I was tired of hearing the broad complain. I got sick of hearing "I'm foul" or "I ain't shit and never goin' be shit." That shit stresses me out. Its bad enough I have to deal with being on the run from the feds. I don't need the extra bullshit.

Listening to my voicemail I heard Beef talking 'bout he locked up, send him money for a lawyer and some commissary. How the fuck did the dumb nigga get himself locked up? This nigga is stupid. What the fuck is he calling me for, they goin' fuck around and trace the call to me. I quickly opened the window of the car and tossed that phone on the Jersey Turnpike, clown ass nigga.

The first thing I did when I got to New York was call Beef's mom. I was at a payphone on a busy Manhattan street when I called her. She relayed Beef's message to me and told me about the charges.

"Murder?" I asked acting as if I didn't know what was going on.

"Tell him to get himself out of what he got into."

We drove to the airport in Queens, LaGuardia to be exact. We pulled up at the lower deck, the arrivals section. I was looking to see if I could spot her. I had a hard time seeing her with all the people coming out of the doors. I got out of the car so I could get a better view.

"F.B.I, don't move!"

"Shit!" Was all I could mumble as swarms of federal agents surrounded me with assault rifles pointed at my whole body. They were everywhere. My run was over.

Once in the backseat of an unmarked Crown Victoria, an agent with a file and an 8 by 10 photograph of me turned and smiled.

"I have to ask you this, Butchie. What made you trust Trish Parker?" That's a question I constantly asked myself. I guess it's the power of the P-U-S-S-Y.

XXXXXXXXXXXXXXXXXX

"I have something very important to talk to you about?"

"How did you get my number?"

"I have my ways, Butchie. Please listen to me...we can't talk on the phone. Where can I meet you?"

Why didn't I follow my first instinct and hang up, get rid of my phone and rid myself of this chick forever.

"Where are you?"

"I'm in Philly.

"Meet me at the 33rd Street station."

I drove up to the station in a rented dark tinted blue minivan. There she was dressed in a white blouse with faded print jeans and a pair of black 3-inch Dior pumps. Her amber colored wig matched the print on her jeans. She looked as if someone punched her in both eyes. They were swollen and red.

"Get in," I ordered as I pulled up to the curb and rolled the passenger side window down. We drove to a cheap motel in North Philly in silence. I didn't wanna speak to her in the car. I had to make sure she wasn't wearing. As soon as we got in the motel room I ordered her to strip.

"Butchie, what is this all about?"

"Strip! I don't know if you bugged, so strip or I'm outta here."

With a reluctant look on her face, Trish stripped. I had to control myself though, that body was still in great shape. She stood there in a red lace matching panty and bra set. Her ass cheeks stuck out from under the panties. Her flat tummy curved down into a slim waist that curved into thick thighs and strong calves. Her D-cup breasts were screaming "suck me," as the bra pushed them up at attention. I grabbed her clothes and searched them thoroughly. In her pants pocket was five thousand in cash, a Black card with the name Derrick Johnson on it and keys. In her Louis Vuitton purse was a picture of her daughter and a Milwaukee driver's license. She was clean.

"What is it you want from me, Trish?" I asked sitting on a beat up flat cushioned chair that sat in front of a small round wooden table by the window. She cried while telling me how Class found the tape on the internet and a paternity test showing that the kid wasn't his. Blah, blah, blah. She went on and on about always having feelings for me and the baby has the same birth mark as me.

"Whatever you want me to do to prove to you that I'm all yours, I'll do it Butchie," she pleaded while hugging me trying to kiss me. I pushed her off of me.

"Hold up Trish. So you just walk away from witness protection and you think them people ain't goin' be looking for you?" Like I said, I should've stuck with my first instinct. They could've followed this broad tryna see where she was going, or they could be looking for her.

"Once you leave without alerting them, they consider you out of the program," she told me. I took her word for it. Why? I don't know, but I put her to the test.'

"Where is Class?" I asked

"Milwaukee," she answered quickly, which explained the Milwaukee license.

"Did they give him a new name?"

"Derrick Johnson. That's his Black card." Damn she really didn't care for this nigga. "If you send someone to get him, don't kill our baby girl!"

"Whoa, slow down. I didn't say I was sending anyone to kill him." I was still a little skeptical of Trish, plus how do I send someone to kill a dude in witness protection without the heat being there. They're probably watching that nigga's every move, especially because he still has to testify at Nafiys' second trial.

I figured I'd deal with Class later on. For now, I had someone else in mind and Trish would be perfect for my plan. Trish and I spent three days in the motel going over my plan and of course some grade a fucking, and Trish still had the skills to make my toes curl as I moaned her name. She even added some new moves in her arsenal of sexual skills. She touched her toes damn near making her head go through her open legs while I hit it. She made her pussy squeeze my rod while her ass cheeks clapped. Wow! Then, she placed me against the wall with my face towards the wall and licked my ass reaching for my man hood at the same time stroking it with massage oil on her hands. I almost screamed out loud that shit felt so good.

We did everything imaginable. I never had an experience like that with any chick, and trust me I tried it all. Trish was the best. Oh yeah, she talked real dirty while it went down.

"I want you to cum on my tonsils, put your dick so far in my mouth that your balls on my tongue." The talk alone would make a nigga bust in 3 seconds.

By the time we were done, she laid in my arms and for the first time I didn't want another man to have her. I didn't want any other man to get that type of sexual experience from her. I wanted her all to myself.

"Yo, lets get married Trish." I couldn't believe it myself when it came out of my mouth.

"Are you serious, Butchie? Yes I will marry you!" She yelled.

"It's going to be an Islamic wedding. You have to be Muslim." I told her.

"Okay I'll do whatever to be your wife."

The next day we went to a masjid in Brooklyn and the Imam performed our wedding. There were only seven people there, Trish and me, along with four witnesses and the Imam. We weren't legally married but in Allah's eyes we were. Trish took her shaha dah (bearing witness to the fact that Allah is God and Muhammad is his messenger). A week later she was in Vegas playing the role of a call girl who was sent to Big Butchie as a birthday present. One night with Trish and Big Butchie was hooked. Of course there's always a glitch in the matrix when you put a plan together. Something always goes off course. Big Butchie was in witness protection. He had an operation to slightly change his face. He secretly kept in contact with me thinking I didn't know he tried to get me to set Nafiys up. He told me where he lived. "Whenever you get a chance, meet me out here so we can do some gambling," Big Butchie told me. He didn't know he signed his death warrant.

There was a U.S. Marshal specifically on Butchie's detail almost around the clock. Big Butchie started constantly using a phony escort service that was really a house Trish had on the outskirts of the city. The agent thought Trish was Big Butchie's girlfriend. When Big Butchie fell in love with Trish, he decided to have a talk with her and he called the agent.

"Sharon. I want you to meet Scott Simmons. He is a U.S. Marshal." Trish who went by the name Sharon, her mother's name, acted as if she was confused.

"Baby, I'm in the witness protection program. There are some people in Philadelphia looking for me," Big Butchie explained the whole story to Trish.

"If you're going to continue a relationship with Butch, you can't utter a word to anyone. If you plan on ever marrying him you'll have to agree to be in the program and have no contact with anyone that means family and old friends." When the agent finished saying his part, Big Butch removed a velvet box from his black slacks and got down on one knee.

"Sharon Jackson, will you marry me?"

Trish covered her mouth with both hands and acted as if she was surprised and happy. Tears formed in her eyes. "Yes Butch, I will marry you!" She hugged and kissed him while looking at the four karat diamond ring with a platinum setting. She wasn't on paper with me, so it was nothing for her to have a private Vegas wedding.

"Butchie, I married him," Trish told me one day from a payphone.

"You did what?" I asked angry and confused.

"I had to, that's the only way I could stay around him. He introduced me to the agent protecting him." Trish explained the whole deal, that's when I realized she was a rider. She went through all that to help me. She is a keeper. I hope she won't be mad when or if she finds out I put another tape out with us having sex. I got a thing for those tapes. I like to watch myself get busy on a chick. Sometimes I perform so well I want the world to see. Of course, she finds a tape we made and she calls me crying.

"Butchie, you goin' fuck our plan up. Why you keep doing this? The Internet! You're going to fuck this up, probably get me killed.

There was another problem, Trish starts going out with the agent. Her rationale for that: "I don't want him to start getting skeptical, so I want him wrapped around my finger."

When she said wrapped around her finger, I knew the extent she would go to accomplish that objective. She didn't have the mental capabilities to do it without sex. There was no doubt using her body was a must to get a man hooked. I don't think there is a man strong enough to resist. Trish a.k.a. Sharon Jackson had Agent Scott Simms wrapped around her finger in no time.

Chapter 17

<u>Agent Scott Simms</u>

"How do you explain your actions Agent Simms?" My lieutenant yelled while I sat in his office the morning after the murder of Big Butch. I wish I had a logical explanation at that point. Saying I was having sex with the witness' wife would definitely get me a quick termination.

"Sir, Ms. Jackson asked me to accompany her to visit her daughter."

"That's inexcusable, Simms. My ass is getting chewed for this, so that means you'll get double chewed!"

"Agent Simms," the lieutenant called before I left his office.

"Yes Sir?"

"How did she wind up at your apartment?"

"Her daughter's babysitter lives just a few houses away from me. On the way back into the city I stopped briefly at my home."

"Why would you bring a client to your home? They're not supposed to know things like that," the lieutenant scolded. I was prepared for all of these questions so all I could do was come up with the best lie I could muster.

"She said she had to use the restroom badly. There wasn't another bathroom around for miles, so I let her use mine." The lieutenant shook his head. I knew there was going to be a big thing about this. There were going to be I.A. investigations, Justice Department investigations and someone was going to be held accountable. The odds are definitely stacked against me. Damn, I messed up. How did I let it get to this point?

XXXXXXXXXXXXXXXXX

A Few Months Back

"Come in here Scott. I want you to meet the lady who swept the old man off his feet," Big Butchie announced to me the night he proposed to Sharon.

Before she came into his life, Butch was a grumpy miserable old man living off of social security and what the government paid him for cooperating. His wife of almost 40 years left him 'cause she didn't agree with the "snitching thing" as she called it. She was a stubborn old woman with more balls than her husband. I had to admit I had a lot of respect for her. Any man who would set his own son up to save his ass was a coward. I hated a coward. I had a job to do, so I acted as if I liked the guy. Honestly, if he didn't have that flaw of being a self-centered coward, I would've liked him. This new girl in his life bought a new glow to his new face. The plastic surgery made him appear a few years younger than his 70 years. When I first laid eyes on Sharon, I was in awe. She is a beauty; she put Naomi Campbell and Beyonce to shame with her looks and body.

"Sharon, this is Scott Simms. Scott, this is Sharon." I couldn't help but to stare at her. I remember clearly what she was wearing. The silk gown by Valentino displayed every curve on her voluptuous physique. She smiled flirtatiously as she shook my hand. Her hands were so soft that I barely felt them in mine. I always got the type of reaction she gave me from women of all roles and nationalities. My 6 foot 3 inch physically fit frame helped also. Women constantly compared me to a dark haired, lighter version of Vin Diesel. If I were bald I'd look exactly like him.

Sharon and I immediately cliqued. She didn't seem like she was as much into Butch as he was into her. Every chance she got, she flirted with me. When Butch took her on a shopping spree, she would ask me how did a particular dress or shirt look on her instead of asking her husband. Butch didn't seem bothered. I figured as long as she was happy and making him happy physically he couldn't care less. Looking at her, I could understand why Butch was sprung. She had this magnetism that a man couldn't turn away from. Every move she made and every time she spoke, it was as if she was inviting you to her sweet smelling body. When she walked in a place, it was as if the Queen of England was there. My only suspicion about Sharon was her accent. She said she was from L.A., but her New York accent couldn't be mistaken as anything else but the Big Apple. For example, New Yorkers rarely called hot dogs, hot dogs. They say franks. What raised my suspicions on that was when she ordered a hoagie from a deli and said, "Let me get a turkey and cheese hero." Hero? That's New York.

Before I could investigate this mysterious woman, one night I found myself playing checkers with her over a few drinks then we were butt naked in Butch's guest room going at it for two hours. Butch was at his psychiatrist dealing with his depression. I never in my life experienced a sexual encounter of that magnitude. My wife had a lot to learn. Sex with Sharon was like an addictive drug. I had to have a fix everyday. Every chance we got we went at it. She made sure not to wear her perfume by Donna Karan when we had sex. I didn't want the smell of a woman on me when I went home at night. The night Butch was murdered my wife was out of town visiting her parents.

"This is a nice house, Scott," Sharon said as she entered the foyer of my Mediterranean style home. She admired the marble white floor leading into a spacious living room with large, woven area rugs. There was a remote controlled fire place, 60 inch plasma t.v. A spiral staircase led up to the second floor where the master bedroom was.

"I didn't know U.S Marshals make that kind of money to afford a place like this."

"We don't. My wife's parents come from old money."

"I guess money can't buy love," Sharon joked while leading me to my wife's king size bed. She pulled my silk tie and slowly undressed me. After I was undressed, she seductively lifted her skirt revealing that she had no underwear on. She leaned back on the bed with her legs hanging off. She looked at me.

"Come fuck this pussy."

There was never a dull moment when it came to having sex with Sharon. The next morning I woke up to a ringing phone and an empty bed. It was my lieutenant. "Simms, get to the office now!" I knew it was going to be trouble, but I didn't think it was this serious. While my lieutenant yelled at the top of his lungs, I was thinking about Sharon. Where was she? Was she alright? Was she alive? Why didn't she wake me up before she left? My questions were answered that night when I received a call from Sharon.

"Scott?"

"Sharon, where are you? They killed Butch, are you ok?" I was concerned. It was good to hear her voice.

"Scott, I can't tell you where I am, it's too dangerous," Sharon replied calmly. She was a little too calm. You would think a woman in her position would be hysterical over the loss of a man who practically gave her the world in such a short time, or at least feared for her own life.

"Sharon, are you involved in this?" I was skeptical. "Oh I see, you used me as an alibi. You're good Sharon, is that your real name?"

"That's not the case, baby, I swear," Sharon said still sounding a little too calm.

"Don't 'baby I swear me'. How long have you or whoever did, been planning everything?" I was pissed off, she was insulting my intelligence.

"Scott, I had nothing to do with this, I swear on my child." Now she started sounding nervous.

"So you're leaving Vegas and the program?" There was a long pause from Sharon. "Yes, I can't stay here. It's too dangerous."

Is she kidding me? She's probably more dangerous than the person who actually pulled the trigger. "All of a sudden you're leaving the program that looks mighty suspicious. You could care less that my job is on the line. I have to answer for this. I know I'm gonna lose my job."

"I'm sorry about all this Scott. It's just a coincidence."

She is good. She could be a hell of an agent. How could she sound so calm and collected about the man she married getting murdered? A guy she was having an affair with was about to lose his job on account of being with her and possibly lose his family if it ever came out, that only heightens my suspicions of her.

"Scott, I'm sorry, but I have to go."

"So that's it. You could just erase what we had and act like it was nothing between us?" I had to ask. When we made love she would tell me how much she enjoys our time together. She enjoyed being around me and was thinking about divorcing Butch for me. I'll admit I was caught up in her lies. I believed that she had a genuine thing for me as I did her.   I didn't even enjoy having sex with my wife anymore. Sex with her was boring and routine once I got to ride the Sharon wave. I found myself falling in love with her.

"I won't erase it. I'll keep it close to my heart." I heard a click then a dial tone.

Before I left my house there was something that needed to be done. I placed a wine glass that Sharon used in a sandwich bag to take to the office. I had to find out about this mysterious woman. If she had a record, which she probably did, probably for prostitution or something, I'd find out who she really was. When I got to the office, I checked the finger prints of Sharon in the NCIC, if she had a record it would be in the system. After a while I didn't find a criminal record on my mystery woman, but what I did fine was a complete shocker. I read the information out loud to myself.

"Trisha Parker the girlfriend/sister of Jerry "Class" Classon, both in the Federal witness protection program. Wait, girlfriend/sister. What the hell does that mean?"

I decided to contact the New York office and see what it's all about. She definitely had something to do with Butch's murder. I'm willing to bet on that. The guy they picked up has all the answers to this puzzle.

Chapter 18

<u>Lavelle</u>

I couldn't refuse an interview with this woman if I wanted to. Damn, Sherry Anderson is a banging chick. When she walked in the studio everybody from my engineers to my female secretary had to do a double take. She didn't walk, she glided in the room. She caught me at the right time. This guy, Pockets, is getting on my nerves with his timing. He wants an album out by the summer, but he comes to the studio anytime he wants. I put up with him 'cause he's cool with my cousin Malik and he's killing the streets with the mixed tapes. Now, he wants to walk in the studio drunk talking about he ready. No, we're on Lavelle's time now.

I walked the gorgeous Ms. Sherry to the lounge area so we could talk. I heard of the magazine and a lot of my artists have been featured in it. They recently did a story on Pockets about his climb to the top of the mixed tape circuit. My cousin, Malik, told me Sherry Anderson tried to interview him about the Black Top Crew, but he refused.

"I'm not telling on myself in no magazine like Cee. That nigga done lost his mind. Jail be fucking niggas' heads up," Malik growled.

Sherry and I sat on a leather couch. Her J. Lo perfume rushed my nostrils as I peeped her strong looking legs. Her black Prada skirt gripped her hips. I felt a tingle in my groin picturing myself in between those thick thighs.

"So, Mister Classon."

"You make me sound old with the Mister Classon. Call me Lavelle, please." That made her show her pearly white teeth. She had an inviting smile.

"Ok, Lavelle. It's a pleasure to meet you. I've met plenty of your artists. They all speak highly of you. I finally get to meet the man behind plenty of people's success. So, how are things on the home front since your father's trial? Did it affect business?"

"Everything is good business wise. The home front, well besides my grandmother's stroke, the home front is tight. I think this whole ordeal has pulled us together. I mean, we're tighter than we were before. We've always been a tight-knit family, but with this experience taught us not to take things for granted.

I don't know if my staring at her legs and things made her uncomfortable, 'cause she didn't show any signs of discomfort. When I stared into her eyes I felt like just grabbing her face and kissing her. I've been around plenty of beautiful women before, but Sherry intimidated me. I've never been that way with a woman. I guess it's because the women I've been around were usually groupies, or money hungry chicks willing to say or do anything to get me to spend on them.

"I'm sorry about your grandmother. I pray she pulls through," Sherry said with a sullen look and voice.

"My grandmother is strong. She'll be fine."

"What's your relationship like with your father since he's been locked up?"

"We talk a lot. He calls my office at least twice a week. I've been real busy so I haven't gone to see him yet. I read his interview with you. I learn something new every day about my family."

I don't blame Malik for being disappointed with my father talking to a magazine. Why would he talk about stuff like that at the same time trying to come home on appeal?

The feds read magazines like *Streets Is Watching*. They know what type of magazine it is. You can't hide anything from Uncle Sam. I'm not in the game so I can't speak on it. To me this is promotion, promotion baby.

"What is your feeling about your uncle testifying against your father?"

"I'm like numb to it, ya know. I felt betrayed by both of them, so that made me numb. At the same time I can't forget what both of them did for me and my family. There's a lot of history there, feel me?"

Sherry nodded her head. I couldn't read her response to my answer. I couldn't tell if she could identify with my reply or if she totally disagreed. I mean I've read the magazine. They definitely don't take kindly to snitches.

"Speaking of history, what do you know about your grandfather, or what have you heard?"

"Ha! Grandfather. Haha!" I had to laugh at that question. I wonder what made her ask that. Her guess is as good as mine.

"Never heard anything about him. In my family tryna get my grandmother to talk about him is like finding the Ark of the Covenant or figuring out the DaVinci code. Never even heard a rumor about the dude. Dead, alive, don't know nothing."

Sherry smiled at me. I don't know what it was about my answer that made her smile, but hopefully she asks more questions I can answer in a way that makes her smile. Hell, hopefully she'll ask me something that my answer could make her take her clothes off for me.

"Your uncle Class is in witness protection and he can't have any contact with you all ever again for the rest of his life. We all know that people in the program do not follow all the rules that U.S Marshals impose. Has he reached out to you or any family members?"

"Besides going to see my moms, no."

XXXXXXXXXXXXXXXXXXXX

After Nafiys' trial I guess my uncle, Trish and the baby were ready for relocation. My sister Tara told me he tried to contact her, about what? I don't know, but she quickly hung up on him. When she told my father that he called, his reaction was "you aint got caller I.D? You could've found out where he was at so I can send somebody at him."

Reckless was all I could say to that statement. My father just doesn't get it. The one thing about Classons, we are some stubborn people. A few days after, Tara told us that a call comes into my office.

"Mister Classon you have a call on line two. He didn't give me his name. He said you would want to talk to him," my secretary said on my intercom.

"Put me through," I ordered. Probably some clown from another record company tryna buy out someone's contract that they wanted from my roster. An artist who owes me two or three albums, but doesn't want to do it 'cause they feel they're being jerked when actually they just can't sell records. When I picked up the phone, the voice I heard felt like a shot of adrenaline.

"Velle, what's happening? Don't hang up on me nephew just hear me out."

I didn't plan on hanging up on him. I definitely wanted to give him a piece of my mind. First I wanted to hear what he had to say. "I'm not going to do that. Plus, I got a bone to pick with you. You got a lot of balls calling any of us after what you just put us through," I said sternly.

Silence.

After about twenty seconds he said "You're right, Velle. I can't argue with you on that point. Trust me man if I could rewind the hands of time none of this would have happened, but the cards were dealt. Sorry won't change anything, I know that. I need ya'll to understand what happened and find it in your hearts to forgive me. I don't want Coco growing up not knowing who her family is."

I'm thinking to myself? Did he think about that before he did what he did? Why all of a sudden did he have an epiphany and want us to forgive him and let Coco continue to be in our lives? What is this dude's agenda?

"I feel for Coco too." I touched on the Coco issue because forgiving him doesn't make things better for me. That doesn't matter to anyone. That baby girl shouldn't have to go through what she's going through. She doesn't understand the whole situation yet, but when she does that could mess her up mentally.

"It's not fair to her or the family. She has to be taken out of our lives due to your inability to face the consequences of your actions. You knew the game and how it comes to an end. You've seen enough and been through enough to know how it plays out. You planned on playing it until you got caught and told yourself you were going to snitch your way out, even if you had to snitch on your own brother. Was that it?" If that's the case, you're really a low down coward and there is no need for this conversation about forgiveness and what's in our hearts. Your heart is what you need to come to terms with."

There, I got it off my chest. I felt like a victim of an asthma attack and I didn't have a pump and someone handed me one. It was a breath of fresh air.

"That wasn't the case, Velle. It's hard to explain. It's hard for you to understand. Truthfully it's hard for me to understand. It's like we all had a plan, a blueprint to this shit. Somewhere along the line, niggas started making their own plans and blueprints without letting me know that they weren't feeling the original plan. A lot of sneaky and underhanded shit came into the equation and it felt like niggas was planning to take me out of the equation."

"Fa real, man.   All that you saying is your justification.   Man, I looked up to you and my pops, more you when it came to swagger and how you do business.   That's where I got my blueprint to run this business.   I'm not like my father.   He handles things violently.   I'm more diplomatic like you were.   I feel betrayed and so does the family.   So un............ I mean Class.   It's too early to be reaching out to any of us.   Let this all sink in and give me time to clear my head of all this madness before any reconciliation can take place.   Give Coco and Trish my love."

"Hold up Velle, don't hang up.   I was also calling about that paper you washed for--"

Click.

He just doesn't stop does he?   Does he actually think I'm gonna hand him two million in laundered money at this point?   He's dead on that.   I donated that to charity, Hurricane Katrina.

XXXXXXXXXXXXXXXXXXXXX

"Nah, haven't heard from him since the trial."

Sherry looked disappointed with my answer.   Did she actually expect me to admit having a conversation with my rat uncle?   A lot of my artists have street credibility they have to sustain, so my label has to hold on to its street cred.

"Before you leave Miss Anderson, I would like to give your magazine an exclusive rap quote from Pockets. This is on his '07 mix tape Death Trap Volume 1."

"It's cool for you to do that for us," Sherry replied.   I got that smile out of her again.   Placing the c.d. in the c.d. player, I turned the volume up so she could hear it clearly. I never seen so many niggas condone rats/of her again/

Talking to ya'll niggas is like having my phone tapped/
This chrome gat/bullets flown at ya bones crack/
I'm a G, you're a G-string you know where the poles at/
Nigga said your block is where all the hoes at/
 I believe that cuz meeting you made that a known fact.
Hold Dat!

Chapter 19

<u>Trish</u>

"Ma'am do you need help with your bags?"

"No I don't." I shouldn't have been so mean to that baggage guy, but he's like the tenth person to ask me that. I know that's how they eat, but the hounding is annoying, especially after getting off a plane. Jet lag is like my period. I can't wait to get out of this crowded airport and get me some serious dick from Lil' Butchie. I'm horny ass hell. Agent Simms' little dick couldn't cut it. I'm tired of faking orgasms. And Big Butchie, I mean the old man was definitely holding, but it took him an hour to get the wrinkly shit up. The nigga's balls looked like some saggy titties on a fat broad. When he finally got hard, his old ass could barley pump. I thought the old fart was gon' die on top of me. Then Lil' Butchie wouldn't have to send nobody to kill him. The things I put myself through for some good loving. What a life.

"Miss Parker?"

"I said I don't need help." Wait, how did he know my name? He don't look like a baggage man. My heart is beating fast as hell now. I know this ain't...

"F.B.I., Miss Parker. You're under arrest." The muscular built agent dressed in tight light blue jeans, some running sneakers and a Giants football jersey spoke calmly. He was accompanied by another agent wearing jeans, running sneakers and a flannel shirt.

"I wasn't leaving the program. I just had to see family!" Damn they hunt people down for leaving the program. I thought they just let you be if you did.

"This isn't about that Miss Parker. You're under arrest for conspiracy to commit murder for hire, forgery and aiding and abetting a fugitive from justice."

I felt my legs wobble and my head started spinning, then everything went blank. When I came to, I rubbed my eyes to focus on where I was. I was sitting in a cell in the New York F.B.I. building. Then I saw a familiar face come to the cell as an officer opened the cage.

"Miss Parker, come with me," Agent Dan Rowland said. I hope his smile meant good news for me like a mistake was made and they were sending me back to Milwaukee to be with Coco and Class. When we got to Agent Roland's office, the first thing he did was hand me the phone off his desk.

"Someone wants to speak to you," Agent Rowland mumbled as he pressed a button to open the line and sat down at his large desk.

"Hello?" When I heard Class' voice I felt like dropping to my knees and letting out a scream. I wanted to beg him to forgive me. I wanted him to tell me, "Trish, don't worry Agent Rowland is gonna look out for me. He has arranged to have the charges dropped against you." Instead, Class grunted.

"Got yo self into some real heavy shit, huh?" He sounded as if he were enjoying my demise.

"Here your daughter wants to speak to you!" Then, my world came crashing in on me.

"Mommy, Hi mommy I miss you." Then it all came out.

"Oh baby, I'm sorry. Mommy is so sor--!" I couldn't even complete a sentence. I cried uncontrollably. Hearing my baby's voice made me realize how stupid I've been. How could I neglect her and put myself in a position to be taken away from her over a man who probably could care less if I ever got out of jail. How could I choose dick over my flesh and blood.

"Mommy, why you crying? Why you not home with me, mommy?"

"Baby I'm crying 'cause I'm happy to hear you. Mommy will be home soon to be with you. I'm going to take you shopping, okay?" I managed to lie between me sniffling and wiping tears with tissue handed to me by agent Rowland who sat there with a blank look on his face. I can't believe I've been away from my daughter for almost 3 months.

After speaking to my daughter, Agent Rowland spoke to Class. He said some things that made me confused, shocked and once it sunk in, sick.

"We have Lil' Butchie and his hit man and they are both talking. You're in lots of trouble young lady. Your daughter will stay with her uncle."

"Uncle? Why can't she stay wit Class?" I know this nigga ain't going to abandon her like that. She knows him as Daddy. Why would he be so mean? Don't mess her life up on account of a broken heart. Damn, I thought Class had a better heart than that.

"She is staying with Jerry," Agent Rowland replied.

"So who's this uncle you talking bout?" I was confused.

Agent Rowland removed an 8x10 photograph from his desk. It was the same picture I saw when me and Class were arrested after the raid on our Long Island condo.

"Remember I showed you this man before?" Agent Rowland pointed to a big man in the picture next to Uncle Bish.

"Yeah."

"He is your father." I stared at the picture for a while, thinking to myself. What does this have to do with Coco and who she is going to be living with?

"His name is Tank. His real name is Keenan Giles. He is also the father of Jerry Classon."

The room started to spin. The words "he is the father of Jerry Classon" echoed in my head. I felt my stomach begin to rumble and then the contents of my stomach rushed to my throat and ended up on Agent Rowland's desk.

When I came to again, I was lying on Agent Rowland's office couch with him standing over me holding a glass of cold water. "Are you ok?" He had a slight hint of concern in his tone.

Am I ok is a crazy question after hearing you've been having sex with your own brother, your own uncle hook you up with, that is just sick. Talk about small world. My world just got super small. The measurement- an 8x10 cell.

"Yes I'm ok?" I lied, taking the glass of water from Agent Rowland. "Does Class know about this?"

"Yes, in fact he was the one who did his own investigation on it. He called me and asked for confirmation once he found out," Agent Rowland said placing his hands in his pants pockets.

"So, you knew all this time?"

Agent Rowland cleared his throat. "It was something we wanted to wait until after the trials to reveal to you both."

"But you didn't. Why?" I asked angrily.

"We didn't expect Nafiys Muhammad to get acquitted of the serious charges. We were contemplating telling both of you after the second trial, but Class got the information from the friendly Internet."

As much as I loathed the thought of being a government witness and didn't want to betray Bish's wish of never becoming a rat, I had to ask a question I pretty much knew the answer to.

"What do I have to do to get out of this situation?"

Chapter 20

Toya

Long Island Jewish Hospital

The last thing on earth I would do is put my grandmother in a nursing home. I don't trust those places at all and no one in the family will go for that. Now that I'm working at Lavelle's label as label president, I have enough time to be a home with her. Since that trial, the already tight-knit family got even tighter. I actually see Malik on a regular basis. He hangs out at the office at least twice a week, mostly flirting with female artists on the label or picking up groupies of some of the male artist. Malik and Pockets, the rapper from Philly that Class brought to New York as a favor for his former friend Nafiys, have become tight. Every time Pockets comes to the city he hangs out with Malik. Even now as I sit in this room with my grandmother who keeps nagging me every 15 minutes to get her something to eat, Malik and Pockets are here.

"Girl, you know I can't eat this nasty hospital food. Go and get me some baked whiting and some real collard greens."

I have to take a cab all the way to Jamaica Queens sometimes 'cause she will only eat fish from one place off Merrick and Linden Boulevard. I like it when Malik is here 'cause he'll drive to the restaurant in his brick red Suburban to fetch my grandmother her food. Tara spends a lot of time at the hospital too. She and Malik have become tighter than usual. Tara got over the fact that Malik dogged her girlfriends. She came to the conclusion that, if they wanted to take the risk after her warning, whatever happens is their fault.

I worry about Malik, though. I'm afraid that he will wind up sharing the same fate as my father. You would think what happened would be a wake up call for Malik, but nooo. He is a Classon and Classons are a very stubborn bunch. I was hoping he would heed my warning:

"Malik, just 'cause I don't work at the parole office anymore that doesn't mean I don't have any contacts. I've got plenty of friends that I stay in contact with and I was told that there is an investigation of your activities, so be careful." One day at the hospital I informed him.

"I'm chillin' Tee." Malik lied. He couldn't even look me in the face when he told me that. Of course, I gave him a look of disbelief.

"Come on Malik, ain't nobody stupid around here. All I'm saying is lay low for a while. You got money. Make it legal. The game is over."

"You're right," was all Malik could say. I don't want to see him fall, but some people have to learn the hard way, and I think my cousin is one of them. I won't give up on him, though.

"You see how things turn out. Look at my father he's talking to magazines now."

"Yeah that's crazy. I can't call why he's doing that."

"It's like he's mad the bitch Tawanna told on him and not me. He's just not using his mind. With all that time they gave him, he's losing it." That was the only reason I could think of why my father would blab his mouth to this magazine. When the lady from the magazine came to interview Lavelle, something I was totally against, she tried to get me to participate and I immediately declined. She should've gone to the courthouse and gotten the trial transcripts. Didn't she hear of the Freedom of Information Act? Anything that didn't come out at trial could be incriminating, and Toya Classon is not into the business of incriminating herself. Believe me, I got some stuff that could send me away forever.

XXXXXXXXXXXXXXXXXXXXXXXX

<u>2003</u>

After two years of working for the state of New York division of parole, I had a full case load of almost 30 felony offenders from various parts of the borough of Queens. I was known around the office as the "Passive P.O" due to my reluctance to sending offenders back to prison for minor infractions such as curfew violation, and arrest for loitering in a project hallway the parolee lived at, along with other petty things that a person wouldn't go to jail for if they weren't on parole. Things ran pretty smooth. With a case load of 30 parolees in 2003, I probably only sent back ten. I got along with most of my parolees. I know how hard it is for a convicted felon to find a job, especially black and Hispanic people. I was lenient and understanding. I treated all of them equally and showed no favoritism. Then in the summer of 2003, I was handed the file of a man named Emmanuel Cross a.k.a Manny Cross."

Manny Cross was the Brooklyn born, son of Panamanian parents who moved to New York before he was born. He stood 6 feet 2 inches tall, medium build, with wavy hair and a bronze complexion that was flawless. He was coming off of a 10 to 20 year sentence for armed robbery. He allegedly held up a check cashing place just a few blocks from the office in Jamaica Queens.

Manny had a criminal record that started when he was only ten years old. Growing up in the Brownsville section of Brooklyn, he started his youthful offenses with petty thefts, vandalism, and a simple assault of a fellow student at his elementary school. Then, at the age of 13 he and a friend held up a laundromat in the East section of Brooklyn. He was arrested and sent to a juvenile lock up in upstate New York where he spent 18 months. He returned to Brooklyn an angry, quick tempered 15 year old on a mission. He wouldn't be on the streets that long. A year later 16 year-old Manny and his cousin, a 15 year-old trouble maker from the Baisley Park projects in South Jamaica, Queens, held up a check cashing place in Jamaica Queens. Besides robbing laundromats and check cashing places, he even held up a church for the worshippers' donations once. He was known as a violent stick-up man of drug dealers, dice games and number spots. He was feared throughout Brooklyn.

His criminal career and his prison record read like a horror novel, multiple stabbings of prisoner, assaults on staff and other infractions that had him in solitary a lot, I was surprised he was paroled before his maximum date. When I finally got to meet this "dangerous man," he was nothing like what his file read. He was soft-spoken and had a humble demeanor. I couldn't see anything about him that matched what his file described. He was charming in a thuggish type of way, clean cut, smelled good, looked very good and expressed his goals articulately and assuredly.

"I received an apprenticeship in heating and ventilation while I was away. I plan on opening my own business once I save enough money from working."

His smile was hypnotizing and I could tell he was in great shape. His short sleeve light blue Izod Polo style shirt revealed muscular forearms with jail house tattoos. His biceps and triceps were in a choke hold by the rims of his sleeves. Everything about him said "Man." Now I've dated men off and on, usually the college educated, white collar type, or one or two guys who worked at the office, but never a thug, especially a parolee. So when I went on a "date" with Manny, I was definitely stepping into unknown territory. It started off with Manny showing up on one of his scheduled visits to my office. He would show up dressed in G.Q mode and made slight advances towards me.

"When did they start tempting brothers by giving them beautiful P.O.'s?"

Of course, I quickly put a dent in his manipulative charm. "Ass kissing won't get you anywhere Mr. Cross, a job and staying out the back of a police car will. That was me putting up a defense, 'cause trust me the sight of this extremely sexy man was an obstacle I had to conquer in order to perform my job in a professional manner.

Then on another one of his visits he shows up wearing a nice fitting suit by Ralph Lauren's Purple label with a Burberry Prorsum Trench coat over it. When he removed his trench coat, I quickly glanced at his gator band watch by Marc Jacobs. On his feet, he wore a pair of black Salvatore Ferragamos to match his suit. He definitely knew how to put it on. Out of nowhere, he reaches in his breast pocket and hands me a purple velvet box. "While I was shopping I saw this in a jewelry store and it reminded me of you. I knew it would look right on you."

"I can't accept gift from my clients. So please Mr. Cross, don't do that."

"I won't take it back," he said with his soft, sexy voice.

His take-charge attitude was a turn on. I love a confident man. He definitely had a lot of guts walking in my office handing me a gift. Knowing that was against department rules. "O.K., I'll take it, but make this your last time doing that."

I opened the box and the most beautiful watch I ever saw sat in it. It was a women's Patek Phillippe diamond bezel, blue diamonds I may add, with a red gator band and red face with roman numerals. It had to be custom made.

"I had your initials put on it. I remember your name from the name plate on the desk. If I knew what the T stood for I would've put that on there," Manny said pointing to my name plate on my cluttered desk.

I'm glad I'm brown skinned 'cause he would have definitely seen the blood rush to my face. "It's Toya."

That sealed it. Next thing you know I'm going to dinner and taking a long walk. Then I'm walking on the Jersey shores with this man who I'm supposed to be supervising since his release from prison.

"Isn't this a violation of my parole?"

"What are you talking about?

"Leaving New York State," Manny joked. In fact, he made me laugh almost all night. He was hilarious and charming. He was a woman's dream when it came to the perfect man. He told me about his upbringing. He was raised in a single parent home in the rough Van Dyke housing projects. "We were poor as hell. We were so poor, even the poor people gave us help."

I couldn't match his story. I didn't grow up as poor as Manny. Though we lived in the projects, we weren't anywhere near poor. My father and uncle made sure of that, but that's something I didn't share with Manny. After two or three dates with Manny, I found myself having multiple orgasms, butt naked sweating like a boxer in the last round of a title fight in various sexual positions in a presidential suite at the Trump Plaza Hotel. Manny's body was so ripped it looked like someone drew him. As Donnell Jones' first cd played, Manny made me feel like I was floating. My body felt like I no longer possessed it. It was all his. His hands, tongue and the enormous appendage between his thighs touched and pleased me in places I never knew could manifest those feelings of euphoria. It felt so good it made me teary eyed.

To reward Manny for his sexual favors, I removed his curfew and increased his visits from once a month to once or twice a week. Of course, he had to visit me at my place or I was at his cozy one bedroom apartment out in Astoria Queens. We spent most of our days watching DVD's and having that unforgettable sex. Every time I had sex with Manny he made me cum, and when I came, the levees in New Orleans would've suffered the same fate Hurricane Katrina brought to them. I could barely walk after our sessions. Any woman knows when a man could bring us that type of satisfaction, he's a keeper. Any fault he has is overlooked when he can perform like Manny. Spending so much time with Manny of course raised red flags amongst my family. My grandmother was the first to make it an issue at one of her Sunday dinners.

"Who is this guy, Toya? You spend a lot of time with this man, but we haven't met him yet. Why? Tell me something baby."

The table, filled with Soul food, got quiet with Malik, Tara, Lavelle, Khalilah and my grandmother staring at me waiting for an answer.

"Yeah what's up with that, Toya?" Malik broke the silence before I could come up with an excuse. "Let me find out he ugly," Malik joked. "Oh I know why. He's one of your clients that's it, aint it?"

Malik really gets on my nerves sometimes, especially when he's right. And my face must've made that clear. "Oh no you didn't Toya!" Tara barked.

"Girl, you done lost your mind. You gon' lose your job messing with that man," my grandmother warned.

"No she won't. Toya know how to play it," Malik said tryna come to my rescue after being the one who hung me out the window by my ankles.

He must be real special man for you to take that risk. You should introduce him to the family," Khalilah commented.

"I definitely wanna meet him. Where he from?" Lavelle snarled. His tone was one of scrutiny.

"He's from Brooklyn." I knew that would role up the room.

"Brooklyn!" Malik growled.

"Oh god girl, I know you ain't 'bout to get involved with one of those people," Khalilah snorted.

"Ya'll act like he's from another planet. What does where he from got to do with it?"

"Dem people are crazy and they thieves, every one of them," my grandmother said.

"Ya'll trippin', like South Jamaica is a good place. There are good and bad people everywhere. Ya'll sound like white people who think all black people are uneducated. Ya'll need to dig ya'll selves," Lavelle preached. He was definitely right. I thought the days of judging people by geographical locations were over. The borough against borough thing is so 80's.

When I discussed the family's Sunday dinner inquest with Manny, he howled in laughter. "People still talk and think like that. It's wild 'cause that stigma is something I carried with me through my time in jail and when I travel to other parts of the city," Manny explained while shaking his head in disbelief.

"I wanna meet them."

Before I introduced him to my grandmother, I first had to get past my father. Once I got past him, everything else was smooth sailing. If he disliked him, there would be a problem.

"He seems like an alright dude. Don't sweat the family talking that Brooklyn stuff. They ain't have nothing else to say," My father tried to reassure me as we talked in his '03 Ninja black Porsche Carrera outside my grandmothers house while Manny sat inside being grilled by the rest of the Classons minus my uncle Class who was out of town.

"Him being a parolee of yours is something you got to be easy with. Is it worth your job?"

"Daddy, he's worth more than that job." I can't believe I was having this conversation with my father about a man I was dating. I never spoke of any man like that before, especially not to my father.

"Daaamn he put it on you!" My father joked.

"Shut up daddy," I said playfully hitting my father on his shoulder.

After the dinner and the family getting to know Manny, I drove him home in my father's Porsche.

"Yo this ride is banging. Your pops and cousin getting money like that, huh?" Manny inquired while looking around the car in admiration. I didn't know how to answer that question without revealing anything about my family, at least when it came to my father and Malik.

"Yeah they got money." Just saying that, I felt like I betrayed my father. I felt uncomfortable and I didn't want to stay on that subject.

"So how do you like my family?" I asked to change the subject. Manny put the seat back almost to the point where he was laying flat.

"You gotta real cool fam. Yo grandmoms is down to earth. She reminds me of my grands."

I was glad to hear that Manny liked my family. They all pretty much liked him too. The only person in my family that was suspicious of Manny was Tara. I attribute that to her untrustworthiness of men in general.

"There is something sneaky about him. He's fine as hell, but he looks sneaky," Tara said to me.

"I met a lot of dudes from Jamaica Queens in jail, especially 40 projects, you know people in 40?" Manny asked avoiding eye contact with me as he spoke. He seemed to be looking off into nowhere.

"That's where my family is originally from. My cousin Malik still lives there," I answered.

Two weeks after that Sunday dinner, I got a call from my grandmother, she was hysterical and panicky.

"Toya come down to Queens General, Malik was shot!" I rushed to the hospital where my grandmother, Khalilah and Corey were waiting in the waiting area. They seemed calm and composed when I saw them.

"What happened?" I asked sounding panicky myself.

"It's cool, he got shot in the foot," my father answered as if getting shot was like having a pimple.

"Who shot him?" My father shrugged his shoulders.

"He said some dudes robbed him in the projects. He tried to grab one of the guys and it went off. They took money out his pocket, his watch and his chain."

Malik was released from the hospital that night. At my grandmother's house, I over heard Malik talking to my father in the bathroom.

"I know who one of those niggas was," Malik mumbled.

"Who, and how do you know? You said they had masks on." My father shot back.

"I recognize that nigga Biz from the Baisley walk and voice. The nigga, Bowlegged Biz Cee."

"Yeah? He just came home he don't live in Baisley no more," my father said.

"Talk to Toya. She can get his address. He's paroled so she can get it."

Of course I did it. Looking up this dude though, I came across some very disturbing information, information I wish I never came across. His name was Barkin "Biz"

Davis. He was the co-defendant and cousin of Manny. During the summer of 2003 Biz and whoever his partner was stayed busy sticking up drug corners and spots all through South Jamaica. Most of the spots turned out to be my father and uncle's spots.

Me and Manny's time together went from being together everyday to just weekends. His excuse: "I've been looking for a place to purchase to start my HVAC business." Of course I was suspicious of Manny. I had a bad feeling he was Biz's mysterious partner in the stickup.

Biz, not able to keep his tongue under control mentioned Manny's nickname in a stick up. One of my father's workers mentioned it to Malik. Malik comes to me with a request. "You can look up in those computers and find out who someone is if there nickname is on file, right?"

"Yeah, if the nickname is on file," I answered.

"Good. Find out about some cat who goes by the name Cross."

My heart hit the floor. I felt a little faint and I needed some air.

"Toya, you alright? Let me find out Manny got you pregnant," Malik joked. This was no joking matter though. The next day as Manny and I lay naked in a Ramada Inn room by J.F.K Airport, I begged him to stop.

"Manny, stop doing what you're doing." We were both lying on our backs while I looked up at the ceiling.

"What you talking about, girl?" he asked turning his face towards me.

"Robbing drug spots," I replied turning my face to his.

Manny jumped up. "Fuck you mean, robbing drug spots!"

I sat up on the bed and held his arm. "My cousin's friend said he heard your cousin, Biz, mention your nickname at a spot ya'll robbed. They don't know it's you. They heard Cross."

"Biz! how Biz name came up in this bullshit?" Manny barked.

"Everybody knows your bowlegged cousin."

"Hold the fuck up. How long have you known that my cousin was supposed to be involved?"

"Manny, I'm tryna stop something crazy from happening to you. My father is not a joke. If he finds out, it will be a bad thing."

"Bitch, what you think niggas scared of yo pops? Niggas aint pussy!" Manny yelled while putting his clothes on.

My heart hurt. I couldn't believe he was coming at me like this. He was a totally different person from my charming prince.

"Bitch! Who you calling a bitch, Manny? I'm tryna help you 'cause you're my man!"

"Your man? Bitch, I'm your parolee and you're in violation. Guess what Bitch, I got us on tape fucking and you sucking me off so open your mouth if you want!" Manny headed to the door once he was fully dressed.

"I'll see you in a month Miss Classon!" Manny slammed the door.

Three days after that dramatic conclusion to what I thought was my knight in shining armor, I handed Malik a piece of paper. Malik read the small paper and then looked at me wide eyed.

"Manny is Cross? Oh shit!" I walked away.

A month later I was removing the file of Emmanuel Cross from my caseload. The *New York Daily* had a article on page 3 that read:

Two men found dead in Brooklyn inferno. Police have recovered the bodies of Emmanuel Cross and Barkin Davis from an apartment in the Brownsville section of

Brooklyn. The apartment was apparently set on fire by someone who tossed a Molotov cocktail, F.D.N.Y investigators say. Police say the two men; Cross a Brooklyn native and Davis of Queens were murdered with gunshot wounds to their heads. Police can't say if the murders were drug related though both victims were recently paroled, violent offenders. If you have any...

This was one of those things my father didn't discuss with my uncle Class. I think my father knew my uncle would be against it, so he said nothing. My uncle never testified about them. I wish things would've been different. I really liked Manny. In fact I fell in love with him.

XXXXXXXXXXXXXXXXXXXXXXXXX

"Grandma, I'll be back tomorrow," Malik said to my grandmother tryna to get out of there because she was giving him one of her speeches as she laid in the hospital bed.

"You think them white folks ain't watchin' you? You make it so obvious that you're still out there. You got these fancy cars, jewelry and a lot of money with no job. Don't be so stupid, Malik."

Malik knows she is right. Of course he took control of the projects once my father and uncle were taken off scene. It's rumored that Malik and his crew are responsible for five murders in 40 in 2006 and they have taken over more territory in Jamaica Queens due to the fall of many crews at the hands of the F.B.I.'s efforts to rid the area of its many drug gangs.

"OK grandma, I'll be here tomorrow. You want me to bring anything?" Malik asked, ignoring my grandmother's speech.

"Yeah, bring yourself to me. Not in a bag or in a cell."

Chapter 21

<u>Class</u>

I feel like I'm on the verge of having a panic attack, so much was is going on in my life in such a short period of time. Every time I come up to breathe, I'm covered by another wave of bullshit. I'm suffocating in drama. There is only one person I can talk to when I start feeling this way. In prison it would have been Bish, but all my life when I was stressing about any issues that came up and I needed some advice I would go to my mother.

I couldn't just pop up at her house or at the hospital due to my current situation so I had to break a rule of the witness protection program. I called her from my Milwaukee home. After she answered on the first ring and we got the "how you doings" out of the way, I discussed everything I had to get off my chest.

"I didn't find this brother of mine, but I found my sister." I wondered if my mother was prepared for the news I was about to reveal. I hope it wouldn't cause a stress induced heart attack.

"It's Trish ma." I heard a grunt from my mother and a brief silence before she said, "I knew she looked like that man. I remember when you told me she was from Harlem. I looked at her closely, but I figured maybe it was a coincidence that she looks so much like him. What about the baby?"

"Coco is not my baby, biologically. Trish has been runnin' around. She is locked up right now. She did some stupid things with her boyfriend." I could picture my mother's facial expressions at hearing this crazy soap opera mess I'm venting to her.

"Oh Lord, Jerry, what is this world coming to? I feel so bad for Coco now. How do you explain to a child all that nonsense, huh?"

"I'm adopting her as my own and when she gets a certain age, I'll explain things. Now, it would just confuse her."

After getting things off my chest to my mother with her advising me to "pray" and "think before you make an irrational decision," I told her that I love her and she would hear from me soon.

The day that I spoke to my mother, I was summoned to a meeting at the F.B.I's Milwaukee office. I figured I would be called to discuss the upcoming second trial of Nafiys. The trial was scheduled for January of 2007. I was escorted by a U.S. Marshal to a conference room with an oval shaped wood table and carpet. A few agents sat with Agent Dan Rowland at the head of the table. Agent Rowland shook my hand as he talked to me when I entered the room.

"Mr. Clas--I mean Johnson, how have things been for you?"

"Besides finding out my girlfriend who cheated on me was really my sister and my daughter isn't mine, I'd say pretty good." Agent Rowland sensed the frustration in my sarcasm. He probably regretted asking me that question.

I fixed my canary yellow silk tie that matched my canary yellow ostrich loafers. Before I sat down at the conference table, I was introduced to the agents at the table. Two of the agents besides Agent Roland were out of New York and the other 3 were from the Philadelphia office.

I was told why there were more Philly agents in attendance.

"The case is being transferred to Philadelphia, Mr. Johnson," Agent Rowland said. "Mr. Muhammad, has been indicted by a federal grand jury in Philadelphia for conspiracy to commit kidnapping and conspiracy to commit murder. Kidnapping is a federal crime and the murder he conspired to, happened across state lines.

"Who did he conspire to kidnap and murder?" I asked. I knew nothing of what they were talking about, so I couldn't testify about it.

"We can't discuss that now. What we want to tell you is that you can only testify to the drugs you had shipped to Philly from New York for Mr. Muhammad," A gruff voiced agent from the Philly office said.

Another long faced agent with a thick mustache removed his wire framed glasses and placed his elbows on the table. "Let me get this straight, Mr. Johnson, you never gave Mr. Muhammad drugs directly? You always had a courier bring it down to his courier?"

"Yes sir," I answered. The agent just nodded his head and looked away. As Agent Rowland started to speak the long faced agent cut him off.

"One more question. Who was your courier?"

"We used different couriers on every trip to avoid unwanted attention from the stick-up man or you guys." In fact there was only one person we used twice to make a trip. I feel no need to testify about that. It ain't that serious. I don't think the dude even knew he was transporting a few bricks of dope.

XXXXXXXXXXXXXXXXXXXXXXXXXX

2004 N.Y.C

"The call me Pockets cuz I'm outta of it into yours/
What u think these lame ass rappers be bitchin for/

Pockets got tha game in the clutch and the figure four /
I'm tha truth and I back it up with proof like liquor store"/

"The nigga is fire, Velle, why he ain't got an album out?" I asked my nephew as me, Lavelle and Nafiys listened to Pockets as he rapped in a sound proof booth at Lavelle's Manhattan studio. Usually there would be an entourage of Pockets' friends smoking blunts and drinking liquor at the studio, but with Nafiys in town, none of that would fly. He wasn't the crowd type and he didn't smoke or drink.

"Yeah he is hot, but he is street hot, not mainstream hot," Lavelle said as he sat at the mix board recording Pockets vocals. "He has to come up with a club banger, a hot single or something to get into the mainstream."

"If the streets love him, eventually the mainstream will get an ear for him. Them white kids love a ghetto story," Nafiys commented.

Puffin on that gank New Yorkers call it that sycamore/
I'm on a yacht, you on tha block scrambling and pitchin raw/
I did it all, grined on the strip to tha brink a dawn/
Now, it's big plates, there a thousand mix tapes that I'm spittin on

As Pockets continued to rap, Nafiys asked to talk to me out of earshot of Lavelle. "You got anybody on hand you can send to Philly now? My man needs two. My peoples waiting on me now," Nafiys mumbled.

"I already sent my horses to the South. Nobody on call right now,"I shot back.

"Class, we done for today!" Lavelle yelled to me. Nafiys and I watched as Pockets came out of the booth and we both looked at each other smiling. An hour later Pockets was on a bus to Philly with a basket ball uniform on, a duffle bag and a brand new Spalding basketball with two compressed kilos of heroine in the ball. Pockets was a hell of a ball player and Nafiys had a team in Philly that played for him all around the city. Pockets was his point guard. "You gotta get down there now. They need you at 16th and Susquehanna," he told Pockets. Susquehanna is a park in Philly where they held tournaments.

"But this ain't the uniform Fiys. What's this about?" Pockets asked about his white and green Celtics jersey and shorts Nafiys purchased.

"You don't want the cops at the bus station harassing you cause you look like a thug. These cops in New York be trippin'."

Pockets successfully got the package to Philly. When he got to the bus station in Philly, he was picked up by Nafiys' people. When Pockets asked about the game he thought he was rushing home to, he was told that is was cancelled because somebody got shot.

The second and last time we used Pockets was when Nafiys sent me a brick of dope to give out samples of and sell if it was good. Pockets traveled to New York with the dope on a bus filled with his fellow basketball team to play at the EBC game at the Kind dome in Harlem.

XXXXXXXXXXXXXXXXXXXXXXX

I saw no reason to tell the feds about Pockets. I felt sorry for the kid. He didn't know what he was doing and he was tryna become a rap star. I'm not going to mess that boy's life up.

"Mr. Johnson, due to this new indictment, we won't be needing you to testify anytime soon. Maybe in a few months we'll be calling you, until then you enjoy yourself. Take a vacation on the government's tab." All the agents laughed at the long faced agent's joke. I didn't find it funny.

Agent Rowland walked me out of the office with his arm around my shoulder. "We'll be beefing up security around you since someone in the witness protection program connected to this case was murdered. The one Trish is charged with conspiring to. To be on the safe side, we're gonna have an agent check in on you everyday and a camera will be installed at your front door. You have ADT, don't you?"

"Yeah I got it."

"It's a helpful tool. I use it myself," Agent Rowland said.

"So can I get that vacation courtesy of Uncle Sam?"

"Sure. Where do you wanna go?" Agent Rowland took his arm from around my shoulder. I acted as if I were in deep thought about where I wanted to go even though I planned to head there weeks ago.

"Arizona"

Chapter 22

Sherry Anderson

Arizona

Every morning I watch CNN and I've noticed every time they show the weather across the country, Arizona is always in the high 90's or reaching 110 degrees. Being here is like being in a sauna as you walk the streets. It is hot like hell. The story I'm doing on the history of the Black Top Crew led me here.

"Is Tank still in witness protection?" I questioned the former U.S. attorney and Mayor Rudy Giussepe on Tank's whereabouts.

The Mayor said that Tank left the program because he felt macho. He isn't scared of the guys he testified against. The Mayor then answered my question about what people like Tank who leave the program do with their lives. They usually return to a life of crime. "In Tank's case, the authorities in Arizona will deal with him."

I learned from the Mayor that Tank was in Arizona. The Internet did the rest. Tank had a phone listed under the name Giles. I'm thinking he definitely has a lot of balls listing his number under his real name knowing men wanna kill him. I called him and he agreed to an interview as he put it, to"clear up any misconceptions and expose a lot of cats that claim to be stand up dudes." Yeah whatever.

When I entered Tank's home in a small desert town a half hour outside of Phoenix, I quickly noticed the measures he took as far as security. I can see why witness protection was not needed for Tank. His one story stone structured home had video surveillance cameras placed on the corners of the house directly under the clay tiled roof. On the screened porch, there were surveillance cameras over the entrance door. The house was surrounded by a black wrought iron fence that was at least 10 feet high and 3 Rottweilers roamed inside the gate. His two car garage also had a camera over it. The security was state-of-the-art. Motion detectors made the lights in front of the house come on when you got within a certain distance of the fence.

Mr. Giles sat on the porch with a shot gun by the wooden rocking chair he sat in. As I approached the gate, he whistled to the Rottweilers and they disappeared behind the house. The gate buzzed and I pushed it open. It was a heavy gate. As I got closer, I noticed that Tank was still a huge man though his age showed on his face. His cheeks were wrinkled and sunken. His once shinny jet black hair was now covered in a low cut style of snow white hair. He wore a white t-shirt with a picture of the co-founder of the Black Panther Party, Huey P. Newton, a pair of faded dungarees and a pair of weathered, scuffed construction boots. A small table held a pitcher of iced water that he had a wooden cane leaning on. He placed a pair of black framed glasses on his face as I walked up on the porch. He stood slowly grabbing his cane for support once I stepped on the porch.

"Miss Anderson, right?" he said in a gruff voice, a voice that sounded as if it had its share of cigar smoke.

"Yes sir. You don't have to stand Mr. Giles."

"Oh no, I know my manners. I stand when a women comes into my presence." That I knew of men in the old days. Chivalry was a macho thing back then. "And you can call me Tank. Tank coughed while he chuckled. "I'm still a young man."

Everybody I've interviewed wanted me to get on a first name basis with them. I mean it wasn't like I was tryna become lifelong friends with these people. I probably would never see any of them again, whether they were in jail or not. Some of them would be dead before I ever laid eyes on them again.

"Tank it is," I happily obliged. "I don't want to take up all of your time Tank. It looks like you were having a peaceful time to yourself." I wanted to make him feel comfortable in my presence so he would open up.

"Oh no. I'm in no rush, take your time. We have a lot to talk about. There is so much you young people need to know about that life, the game."

I sat on a rocking chair juxtaposed to Tank's that had a small coffee table between them. I placed my recorder on the table and began my interview.

"You were a legend in Harlem, Tank. Harlem was your world, what do you miss about the old neighborhood?"

Tank had a grin on his face and he gazed out at the sky as if in deep thought. He had the look of a person gazing back in time.

"I miss the 'go get it' atmosphere. Harlem is a place where if you're not chasing whatever it is you're tryna get to, you will never see it again. It's fast; it's a hustla's heaven and a punk's nightmare."

"I have to be blunt, Tank. This is what this magazine's about, realness and the facts." I could tell by his change in posture (he sat straight up) that he knew where I was going next.

"Do you regret becoming a snitch for the government? If you have no regrets about it would you advise a guy in the game right now to do what you did in your situation?"

"No regrets," Tank spoke confidently. "Honor and loyalty are like newspapers, you read it in the morning on your way to work, then throw it away ten minutes after you bought it. It's superficial to the cats in the streets, it aint in their hearts. So how could I regret turning on cats who turned on me. I got even."

"People say that's an excuse to do what was already in your heart. If the guys you run with break the code that you all swore to, why would you stoop to their level instead of remaining real to yourself and roll with the punches?"

Tank stared at me while folding his hands on his lap. "Do you want something to drink?" he asked politely. "I got some ice cold tea in there. I also got some corn liquor. You don't look like the corn type," Tank chuckled.

"I'll have some tea, thank you."

"Ok." Tank didn't move. He just sat there. A minute later a petite pretty, young Mexican woman walked out of the house with two glasses of iced tea on a silver tray. "Gracias, Penelope," Tank said grabbing the glasses handing me one. The woman went back in the house. He has someone watching the porch from inside the house. Yeah Tank is a very security minded man.

"I did roll with the punches, Miss Anderson, but a man can only take so many blows to his body. You eventually break down. My strength and weaknesses aren't the same as another man's. Every man has a different breaking point. And I'll tell you this, jail wasn't mine-- betrayal was."

"What do you say to the men and women in prison right now, betrayed by their friends and even family members who didn't become a government witness?"

"I applaud them," Tank clapped his hands with a stained teeth smile.

"I'm not making excuses for my actions. I said I have no regrets. I wouldn't advise anyone to take the route I took. The way I'm living now, having to watch my back from people who wanna kill me for whatever reason, is the same way I had to live when I was in the game. So a person coming into this life has to ask themselves if it's it worth it.

I never asked myself that question before I got in the game. The only question I asked is how much money can I make and where to spend it all."

"Tank, I'm doing a story on a crew known in New York as the Black Top Crew out of the Southside of Jamaica Queens."

"I met a couple cats in the feds from out that way, some real cats. Ronnie, Bumps and Tommy. Some real money makers out in Queens," Tank interrupted.

"I'm sorry Miss Anderson continue."

"This Black Top Crew was headed by two brothers with the last name Classon." I looked at Tank's face for any expression of recognition at the mention of the name. He dated so many women and had kids by a few that he probably doesn't remember Class and Corey's mother Phylicia.

"My research led me to the mother of these brothers whose name is Phylicia."

Tank looked down at his folded hands and then grabbed his glass of iced tea and took a long gulp downing the whole drink.

"Put a little Vodka in there to loosen up."

"Do you remember Phylicia?"

"Yes I remember Phylicia Classon from down South. She had three kids by me and left Harlem. I never saw her again or the kids."

"These boys who headed the Black Top Crew are your sons. The girl you had with her died of an overdose." I watched as Tank sighed. I remained silent for a few seconds to let what I said sink in.

"The F.B.I brought the Black Top Crew down and your son, Jerry turned government witness against his brother Corey. Corey is serving life as we speak."

Tank stared off into the Arizona horizon leaving me to wonder what he was thinking. I wondered if he thought testifying for the government was something he passed on in his genes. Was he thinking he had a genetic weakness that he was a coward and it flows through his blood, or was he thinking about being a father who abandoned his children who chose the wrong path because they didn't have a positive father figure causing them to be bitter with the street life being a direct result of that bitterness? Was he sad that his oldest daughter died of an overdose of a drug he once help flood the streets of Harlem with? Was he feeling the weight of all the dead people who overdosed on the heroine he sold? I hope he was thinking those things, cause I damn sure was.

"I wrote her letters, she never wrote me back. I called and she hung up and never accepted my calls. I wanted to be there for the children, but she wouldn't let me," Tank said with a sad voice.

"How do you feel about what I relayed to you about your sons?" I wasn't going to let him avoid that topic.

"I could easily sit here and blame myself for not being there for them, but is that really the reason they sold drugs or did whatever crimes they're in jail for? I doubt it. Many good parents are dealing with children who rebel and do the wrong things. Society has to take the blame also. It's more of a culture thing than anything else. This country is based on materialism and capitalism. They focus more on monetary gain than education and intellectual gain. Sex, drugs, cars and clothes are at the forefront of American society and these kids do whatever to get those things. Just listen to the music they got out there now."

Tank definitely had a point. I can't argue with that, but it's still not an excuse to walk out on your children or cheat on your woman. "Education starts at home, Tank, do you agree?".

"Of course I do. But, do I deny my children television, do I deny them the freedom to play with their friends in the streets, do I not go to work so I can stay home and watch everything they do? If I can't afford to send them to a private school, do I deny them a public school education, a system that cares less if our Black and Latino children learn anything, a public school where the kids are faced with peer pressure, where they're exposed to drugs, sex, guns and violent rap lyrics? Let me know when you want me to stop 'cause, Miss Anderson, it's a cold world and it ain't getting any warmer."

I see why he agreed to this interview. This man has a lot on his mind. He probably doesn't have any friends or people he could talk to. The Mexican woman probably can't speak English and could care less what this old paranoid black man has to say. Her biggest worry is probably the Immigration Naturalization Service.

"So how is Phylicia?" Tank changed the subject.

"She just came out of a coma from a stroke." I removed a picture that I received from a person Tank and I both knew from my purse and showed it to him. Tank stared at the old black and white photo for a few seconds.

"The old gang. We were the jazziest cats cross 110th Street. That's Bish, Guy, Ricky, Frank and me at the Apollo."

"Tell me about those days... Phylicia and the gang, share that with me."

XXXXXXXXXXXXXXXXXXXXXXXXXXXX

<u>1966, Harlem</u>

"That's a fine country girl you got there, Tank. I see you put something in the oven again. What you plan on doing, settling down?" A friend of Tank by the name of Guy heckled as he, Tank and a couple of their cronies shot craps at a gambling spot in the smoky basement of a bar on 138th and Fredrick Douglas.

"That's why I'm going to take your money with this dice. Child support, blood, get him!" Tank barked while throwing two red die across a pool table.

"Point. Pay up!"

Guy and other men in the game handed Tank cash and jewelry from off their wrist and hands. "Her country friend is a fine dame. Tell your woman to tell her partner to give a brother like me some well needed attention." Guy smirked after handing Tank his money.

"I don't think that dame likes hard meat. I think she a vegetarian or she just eats fish," Tank shot back.

"She just ain't had a playa like Guy in her life," Guy boasted in third person. He was known in the crew as the pretty boy. He prided himself on the fact that women around Harlem knocked each other over to flirt with the light skinned, hazel-eyed, curly-haired playboy who was also a street ball legend throughout the city.

"You were using another name when I first met you, am I right?"

"Yeah I was, but my momma always called me Sharon."

Tank and Sharon laid in each other arms drenched in sweat after a 4 hour bout of sexual aggression in his queen size bed on top of burgundy satin sheets. They stared up at the mirrored ceiling at their glistening silhouettes.

"Why Sharon?"

"It's my middle name. Marquita Sharon Burgess."

Marquita, born and raised in New Orleans moved to New York in 1958 a few years before she met Phylicia Classon at City College. Marquita was the one who convinced Phylicia to take up black studies at the college. "If we don't learn about our past, we will never be prepared for our future," Marquita advised.

When Phylicia started dating Tank, it was Marquita who protested against the union. "Those New York men are nothing but two timing playas." Phylicia dated Tank despite Marquita's advice. But while Tank courted Phylicia he also charmed his way into Marquita's bed.

"There was a time you hated New York men, why the change of heart?" Tank asked Marquita while playing with her one braid by her temple with the rest of her hair in an afro.

"Phylicia must have told you that." Marquita rubbed Tanks huge chest.

"She mentioned it," Tank replied.

"I didn't like New York men for the same reason we're lying here naked. Ya'll all gigolos."

Tank laughed at the irony of Marquita's statements. "So why are you here with me?"

"This city has corrupted me," Marquita chuckled.

When Phylicia found out Tank was having a son by another woman and decided to leave Harlem, Marquita was by Phylicia's side lending moral support.

"I told you Phylicia, that man was no good. It's hard to find a good man in Harlem," Marquita snarled as Phylicia packed her and her children's clothing and other belongings.

"That's why I'm leaving Harlem. This place will drive me crazy. That man will never see me or these kids again," Phylicia growled.

Marquita was elated. "That's right baby, to hell with Tank." With Phylicia out of the way, Marquita could enjoy her love life with Tank. As hard as Marquita tried not to fall in love with Tank, she eventually did.

Tank loved Marquita, now known to everyone in the neighborhood as Sharon, but he wasn't deeply in love with her as she was with him. Tank had lots of women at his disposal, and to him they all had a purpose. He used women for sex, and their apartments as stash houses. He used Sharon's apartment as a cut house. He used Sharon to recruit women to cut and package the dope. Sharon became the first and only female who hung out with the crew. She was practically part of the Counselors. Tank had her believe that she was his main chick, but that thought was quickly erased when Sharon did her own detective work on Tank. She knew he slept around with a lot of women before they became an item, but she thought she changed him. The woman Tank had his son by lived two blocks from Sharon. Tank told Sharon the he didn't deal with the woman on a relationship basis.

"I just dropped in to see my son," Tank lied.

Sharon followed Tank one night after he left her apartment. He walked the two blocks to his son's mother's apartment. To Sharon's dismay, the woman was standing in front of the building dressed to hit the town. Her white fur reached to her ankles and her diamond earrings lit up the Harlem night. Sharon's heart dropped in her brassiere as she witnessed Tank hug and French kiss his son's mother long and passionately. Then Tank walked to one of his Cadillacs he left parked in front of the building and opened the passenger door for the woman. He waited for her to get in the car before he ran jovially to the drivers side.

"He don't hold doors open for me," Sharon mumbled to herself.

Sharon walked back to her apartment enraged. She thought long and hard about how to get payback. Then, she came up with an idea. Sharon decided to do a thing that made her run from New Orleans, Voodoo magic. Something she learned from her mother, a practice that scared the hell out of her. She remembered a spell that her mother cast on her cheating father. Marquita's mother cast a spell on her husband's genitalia. He was never able to get an erection ever again.

Sharon took a picture of Tank and placed it on a homemade altar. She went outside of her building and walked to an alley beside it. She spotted what she was looking for as soon as she entered the alley, a cat. In one hand she held a can of tuna, while calling the cat "pst, pst come here kitty kitty." The cat ran over to Sharon. She placed the can of tuna on the cracked and littered pavement. The cat quickly started devouring the tuna. In her other hand that she had behind her back was a meat cleaver. With one swipe Sharon hit the cat with the flat side of the cleaver knocking it unconscious.

She carried the cat up to her third floor apartment and placed the unconscious cat on the altar. She chanted some Creole words over the picture of Tank and the cat. She lit a few candles circled around the altar then she chopped the cat's head off with the meat cleaver. She held the cat up by the tail and let the blood drip on Tank's picture. While she continued her Creole chants. The spell she cast was a curse on Tank's children. The spell was that Tank's children would grow up not knowing who he was and hating him forever, her other vengeful act, sleeping with his friend and fellow Counselors member, Bish.

XXXXXXXXXXXXXXXXXXXXXXXX

2006

"I was told that you were tricked into thinking that Bish and Sharon were related. How did they convince you? I asked Tank.

"They actually were related through marriage. They told everyone they were brother and sister. Sharon moved from the South to be reunited with her family. That's what they told everyone. I met her at the cotton club with

Phylicia, but I was introduced socially to her through Bish. They fooled us all, I'll tell ya."

This whole story is like a novel. I should write a book about this instead of putting it in a magazine. This would definitely be a bestseller. This can be a soap opera too. So much betrayal and back handed bullshit.

"Miss Anderson, I have so much more to tell you, but I'm a little tired now. You can come back tomorrow. I'll pay for the hotel expenses if you like," Tank proposed.

"That'll be fine with me Tank, thank you."

Tank got me a room at a Phoenix Best Western. I went straight to bed when I got to the room. I woke up the next morning, showered, applied my make up, nothing heavy just some MAC eye liner and lip gloss, and pulled my hair into a ponytail. I went to the hotel restaurant and had a breakfast of cheese eggs and sausage.

"What does a person do for fun in Arizona?"

I heard a deep voice as I ate my breakfast while looking at a copy of *The Wall Street Journal*. I looked up and saw a tall, well-built, well dressed handsome black man standing there. He had a soft, sexy voice, but manly at the same time.

"I wouldn't know. I'm not from Arizona," I said wiping my mouth with a napkin.

"That makes two of us. I'm, sorry for interrupting you. I'm on vacation and I was just wondering what to do on my stop in the hot state."

"I was just checking the market, you weren't interrupting at all." I can't believe I said that. I have no time for another man in my life. I'm happy. A little flirting won't hurt, though.

"Is this seat taken?" he asked referring to the empty cushioned seat in the booth I sat in.

"No it's not." He sat across from me and sipped from a straw on his cup of sparkling water.

"Where are you from?"   I was always in interview mode.

"I'm originally from New York, but I currently live in Wisconsin."

New York? That's a coincidence, but then again I'm not surprised. Every where I travel I run into a New Yorker, we are everywhere. People who aren't from New York run to visit the city, but the people who are born and raised there run from it.

"What Part?"

"I'm from uptown," he answered. "You?"

"The Bronx" I answered with my best Bronx accent. I loved the way it sounded when I mentioned my beloved borough. The only place I know that has the definite article in its name. It made the place sound unique. And to me the Bronx was unique. Yeah the boogie down.

"My name is Sherry. I'm in Arizona on an assignment. I'm a journalist."

"Yeah? That's what's up.   For a newspaper or magazine?" he asked curiously

"I write for a magazine called the *Streets Is Watching*. I'm doing a story on street gangs." I lied. I don't like telling a person about my story because I want them to purchase the magazine instead of me giving up the goods.

"I read it a couple of times. Excuse my rudeness. My name is Derrick.

Derrick and I talked for a half hour about nothing of importance. He shared his view on street gangs with me. We talked about places in the city we both were familiar with. I told him it was nice meeting him. I had a story to finish. He said the feeling was mutual and wished me a safe trip back home. I declined taking his number or given mine. One thing was for sure, Derrick was fine.

My interview with Tank was scheduled for the afternoon, so I spent the day going over my draft of the Black Top Crew story. I couldn't put everything I recorded in the magazine. I had to edit and delete stuff that had nothing to do with the actual story we were trying to get out. By 12:30 in the afternoon I was on my way to see Tank. I drove my rented nave blue Chrysler 300 to Tank's fortress. Once again it was close to 100 degrees, so I wore a white tank top, a pair of sky blue linen slacks and a pair of open toe Gucci sandals.

When I pulled up in front of Tank's home, I parked my car in the drive way in front of the garage. Tank sat on the screened porch and from where I sat I could see the silhouette of another person, but not the face. The person's back was facing me. After being buzzed into the gate, I headed towards the porch. Tank opened the screen door and I was able to see his guest sitting with him.

"Miss Anderson, you wouldn't guess who showed up this morning," Tank said excitedly. Derrick stood up with a pearly white smile.

"Sherry, we met this morning. What's up?"

"Hey Derrick, what brings you here? I asked a little confused. Why was Derrick sitting on Tank's porch, why would a guy form New York who says he's on vacation be visiting Tank? Maybe Tank is still in the game on the down low.

"Small world, isn't it? This is my son Jerry. I was telling him about our conversation yesterday," Tank said. I couldn't hide my excitement. Oh wow! Class?

Chapter 23

<u>Nafiys</u>

Bang! Bang! Bang! Who is knocking on my door like the police this early in the morning? "Baby, you expectin' somebody?" Ryan asked wiping the cold out of her eyes.

"No baby, go back to sleep I'll get it." I got up and put my white cotton robe on. Before I got to the French double doors of our bedroom, I heard the cocking of a gun. I turned to look back and there was Ryan in her silk nightgown holding a Glock 40 by her side.

"I'm going with you," Ryan mumbled. She reminds me everyday of why I fell in love with her.

When I got to the door and looked out the peephole, I saw two suited white men who couldn't be mistaken for anyone else but the feds. I opened the door with a confused look on my face. I didn't do anything wrong like leave town without permission. I haven't been in the presence of criminals, but like twice since I been on the streets and that was when I went to South Philly to see Lil Butchie before I found out what he did to my brother. The other time I was with my family at the masjid in the company of a lot of criminals that attend the masjid in Germantown. I looked at my ankle monitor to see if something was wrong with it. It was the same as it always was.

I opened the door after telling Ryan the cops were here. "It's the police. Go in the room." Once I opened the door, the agents flashed their badges.

"Mr. Nafiys Muhammad?" One of the agents said.

"Yes. What's the problem?"

"Mr. Muhammad, we're placing you under arrest. You have the right to remain silent anything you say…"

"What is this about?" I yelled causing Ryan to run towards me.

"Now what, what he do now! He's been home for weeks. What are ya'll arresting him for?" Ryan cried.

"Baby, call Shabazz, tell him to get downtown!" I ordered Ryan.

"What's this about, sir?" The agent was still reading me my rights.

"If you cannot afford an attorney, one will be appointed to you. You also have a right to waive your rights and give a statement."

"What are ya 'll arresting me for?" I yelled.

The agent stop reading me my rights and the other agent while lacing his cuffs on my wrist said: "you have been indicted by a federal grand jury for conspiring to kidnap Khadijah Bint Shabazz and conspiring to murder Butch "Big" Samson."

Hearing a thud, I turned to see Ryan looking at me in shock. The thud sound was Ryan dropping her cell phone. Hearing everything the agent said Ryan with tears in her eyes screamed out. "Tell me that isn't true Nafiys, not Khadijah!"

It shocked me to see Ryan lose her cool. "Baby, they got me mixed up or somebody's lying! Just call Shabazz."

During the ride downtown, I thought about what or how Shabazz would react once he saw the charges I've been indicted on. From what I hear, Lil Butchie got pinched and most likely he is running off at the mouth to save himself. I wish he could have been found before he got pinched. I told the clown I'd handle Big Butchie, but he goes right ahead and sends somebody to Vegas after I already sent someone. Good thing I didn't tell anyone I sent Pockets to off Big

Butchie or he'd be caught up in this mess. Pockets got there before Beef, and whatever chick Lil Butchie sent down there to set Big Butchie up was just leaving the house he was in and Pockets slid right in.

"Yo Fiys, I sat parked in a rent-a-car for like a week straight at the corner of Big Butch's dirt road block. The block was so empty I was able to pull it off without being seen. Man that car was funky. I shit in a box and pissed in a two liter sprite bottle. I couldn't even take the smell of myself."

Pockets told me all this once he returned to Philly and we met up in North Philly. Pockets was a soldier. He's loyal and I pray he never gets caught up in this mess.

I hope I can convince Shabazz that the kidnapping jawn ain't true. There isn't a lawyer like him that I know of. Shabazz is a true die hard defense attorney who will go all the way for his client regardless if the client is guilty. Shabazz does his job as if he believes everyone he represents is innocent. I know I can most likely beat the charge cause the cat who kidnapped Khadijah won't open his mouth. Lil' Butchie's credibility ain't nothing, hopefully a jury will see that. Shabazz can make a jury see it my way. If he is still my lawyer, when it's all said and done.

When I got downtown, I was booked and processed. I was escorted to the attorney visiting room. As soon as I entered the room I saw the redness and puffiness in Shabazz's eyes. He had a stack of paperwork in his hand. When I got close to the chair to sit, Shabazz remained standing. I saw tear stains on his gray Temple University sweat shirt. Then he launched the stack of papers at me. They hit me directly on my face. I turned away for a quick second to try and dodge them but they hit me on the chin and then Shabazz lunged at me attempting to choke me.

"You snake motherfucker. My daughter, you son of a bitch!" I grabbed Shabazz's hands and tried to wrestle him to the ground, but I underestimated his strength. He pushed my hands off his arms and threw a hay maker with his right hand. I ducked it and hit him with an upper cut to the rib cage. I heard him grunt before he attempted to throw anther hay maker with his left hand. Again, I ducked and threw a two piece combination, a hook to the body and a straight left hand to his chin. As he was dropping from the punch, two agents ran in the room and rushed me to the ground. Another agent grabbed Shabazz and escorted him out of the room. I was placed in a small odor filled cell until I saw a judge who revoked my bail for the charge I was on home monitoring for and gave me no bail on the new ones. Things just went from bad to worse.

I was sent to the Philadelphia Federal Detention Center and placed in administrative custody. I had to be separated form Lil Butchie, Beef and the cat who killed my brother. They were all in the detention center also separated from each other.

There were a lot of dudes in the cell block I was on from Philly mixed in with dudes from other parts of the country that were on what they call "the Wheel," convicts who are being transferred to different prisons all over the country. Some of them have been on buses and planes for months only to stop at a facility for a day or two, even a week to eat, shit, shower and shave.

"Hey Fiys, that's you baby boy?" someone yelled. I couldn't recognize the voice. I wasn't into getting on the cell door and yelling across the tier. Dudes in prison like to listen to other people's stories and either lie that they know you or run to the cops and rat you out. In jail, it's called "ear hustling." Still, I was curious to know who that was.

"Yeah it's Fiys, who dat?"

"You don't know me dawg. I'm from Mill Creek. Listen I gotta holla at you homey. Play the yard in the morning."

"If we don't know each other then what we got to holla about, I'm not on no Joe familiar crap playboy!" I guess I got under this dude's skin by calling him Joe familiar in a subliminal kind of way.

"Why you calling me Joe familiar? Listen nigga, yo peoples killed my cousins in Mill Creek. Pussy I'mma see yo ass!"

"You had to yell that on the gate nigga. You could've just kept your mouth closed and did what you had to do!" I responded. This is the main reason why I don't stand on the cell door yelling to other inmates. If I got beef with you, I'm not going to announce it to the world, scared niggas do that. If I'm talking to a homey, I'm not putting my or his business on air. The guy with the threats kept running his mouth. I just ignored him and decided to let the call for yard be the bell. I lay down on my bunk unsure of my future, one thing for certain is I had to get a top notch lawyer to take my case. Without Shabazz on my side, things could go crazy. I know there's a lot of good lawyers in Philly but Shabazz is good friends with all of them and he could black ball me. The kidnapping of their colleague's daughter is goin leave a bad taste in their mouths. You shit outta luck when you leave a bad taste in the person's mouth you need to save your life.

The next morning I was awaken out of my sleep by a guard banging on my cell door. "Muhammad you gotta visit!"

After I washed up and got dressed, I was escorted to the visiting area. The brown skinned female officer who escorted me to the visiting room flirted with me all the way there. "They lock up good men everyday out here. Maybe if a good woman was in your life you would stay home."

She fluttered her eyelashes at me with a smile on her round chubby face. I ignored her. I had the best woman a man could ever ask for. I wouldn't trade her for Megan Good, Sanaa Lathan or the beautiful Lauren London. It felt good to see Ryan sitting there in the visiting area. What I didn't understand was why she wasn't wearing her head covering. A Muslim woman is supposed to keep her head covered in public or in the presence of non family members. Ryan didn't look happy to see me.

"As Salaamu Alaykum," I greeted her. She didn't look me in the face or stand to greet and hug me.

"You're not going to hug or greet me, Ryan? Don't embarrass me. Stand up greet me and hug me. I never disrespected you," I mumbled between grinded teeth. She changed my mood with her actions. I went from happy to see her to ready to walk away from her forever in one second. Still avoiding eye contact, Ryan stood, hugged me quickly and sat down. "What's your problem?" I saw the tears well up in her eyes as she replied.

"I can't keep going through this Nafiys. It's like I hardly know you. Just when I thought I did, I hear this? You're evil Nafiys."

"Don't you understand these people are tryna set me up, how can you just lose faith in me that fast? You act like they have proof that I did that."

"Obviously they do!" Ryan snapped.

A lot of people don't realize that the government will go to any length to get a person off the streets that they feel is getting away with crime, especially a black man, we're not suppose to win cases. The criminal justice system wasn't made for that. This system is a continuance of the enslavement of black people and poor people. I'm not supposed to own businesses in my neighborhood; I'm not supposed to give jobs to people in the ghetto. They are supposed to depend on the government for assistance. I'm not supposed to give jobs to young black men to support their families. The young black man should be dead or in jail while his family struggles to make it. I'm supposed to be subhuman, if not, the white supremacists are proven liars and history books have to be rewritten.

"Just like they had evidence before, right Ryan?" I grunted turning Ryan's face to look me in the eyes.

"Shabazz won't talk to me, neither he nor his wife. They won't even look at me. I saw them at Jumuah and they walked right past me like I was invisible. Then everybody at the Masjid was giving me dirty looks. I had to leave, Nafiys," Ryan cried. Why would they do that to her.? They know me. Even if I did do what they're accusing me of, they know me well enough to know I wouldn't discuss that with anyone, especially Ryan. She wasn't even my woman when Khadijah was kidnapped.

"It isn't your fault Ryan that people are ignorant."

Ryan wiped her tears with a napkin then she stared at me almost menacingly. "I'm not mad at them. I understand why they feel like that. It's 'cause of you. My husband is a monster and I know he's one. They are not ignorant, Nafiys. You are!" Ryan stood up and threw her napkin on the table in front of us. "I won't take your son from you, Nafiys. I hope you make it through this, but I won't be waiting for you outside the prison or courtroom. Good bye!"

My heart hurt as I watched the love of my life walk out of that visiting room, possibly out of my life forever. She is the last person I wanted for this to turn out this way. I needed her and my son by my side. I needed to hear her say baby you're going to come out of this. I needed to look out in the courtroom and see Ryan with my son, mouthing she loves me while I'm on my way to spanking the case. Damn karma isn't a joke. I just pray Allah forgives me. When I returned to the cell block, I was quickly reminded of why jail stresses me out. "Yo Fiys, what you scared nigga? I was waiting on yo ass in the yard, playboy. You ain't shit without your team, huh pussy?"

I was too stressed to feed into this dude's bullshit. This clown is miserable. He wants me to be as miserable as him and yell on the cell door all day. The cell block is locked down for 23 hours a day. It's a block for high risk inmates who haven't been cleared by security to enter the general population. So, to kill time some guys start arguments with other inmates, the arguments last all day, even into the next day. I ignored my nemesis and told myself that I'd deal with him the first chance I got.

The next morning after breakfast, we were let out into the small yard that consisted of one basketball hoop, a pull up bar and dip bar. You can smell the tension in the air once the cell doors open. I didn't know who the guy was. I never got a chance to see him. I felt at a disadvantage because of that fact. I expected the loud mouth to be yelling obscenities once the gates cracked, but there was nothing but the sound of cells buzzing open and keys jingling as the guards escorted us out into the yard. I scanned everyone's faces for familiarity and to see if any of them gave me the murder one stare. No familiar faces and no menacing stares. When I entered the yard, I immediately put my back against the wall so no one could sneak up behind me. A few cats ran to the court while other strolled the yard with other inmates. There was one wooden table where a few dudes went to play cards. Then out of nowhere something smelly and stinky was tossed on my face. Whatever it was blinded me and soon started to burn.

"Hold that, you bitch ass nigga!" I heard that voice barking. It was my enemy. I heard the sound of the guard's keys running in my direction as I grunted in agony holding my eyes. I realized I got gassed. Gassed is when an inmate tosses his feces and urine mixed in a cup or jar that most likely was sitting for a few days into someone's face. It's one of the most humiliating things that can happen to you while in jail. I definitely felt humiliated. I felt the guards holding me pulling me back into the block. "Keep your eyes closed Muhammad!" a guard advised me. Though I was keeping my cool, I was furious. In my mind I was saying. When I find out who this dude is, I'm going to have his whole family killed. And when they kill them I want them to have feces and urine thrown on their bodies. I'm glad my mouth was closed when the concoction was tossed in my face, that would've been some messed up stuff. One thing was certain, this guy is in the federal system and any jail he goes to I can get him touched so he better lay as low as he can. He is going to get it.

Once I was cleaned up and given shots, just in case the guy was carrying something, I had to get down to business. I had to find a lawyer. I called a friend of mine who ran one of my Halal meat markets in west Philly to get me nothing but the best. "He doesn't have to be from Philly. They got good lawyers in Harrisburg, Chester and other parts of PA. Get on that A.S.A.P."

In the meantime, I was moved to another unit in the jail. This unit was quiet and it housed inmates who were waiting to get deported back to their countries or fighting deportation. I couldn't even find out who the guy who gassed me was. Lucky for him though. When I do find out, he's going wish he never crossed paths with Nafiys Muhammad.

Chapter 24

THE UNITED STATES OF AMERICA vs. NAFIYS MUHAMMAD

Sandra Weinstein, Esquire

    Month after month, I reviewed the discovery package that the government turned over to me. I prepared opening arguments and summations, interviewed Mr. Muhammad and witnesses I planned to call. After going through the stress of fighting to get a jury that would not be biased towards my client, I was ready to go to trial. It could last more than a month.

    Excuse me reader, allow me to introduce myself. My name is Sandra Weinstein, that's Mrs. Weinstein, esquire. I'm a 30 year old Jewish-American woman with six years of law experience under my belt. I know that's a short time, but in that short time I've managed not to lose a case. I graduated from Harvard law school and hold a masters degree in economics. I also have my own accounting business in Philadelphia. I was born and raised in Northeast Philadelphia by Jewish parents who moved to Philly from the slums of Williamsburg, Brooklyn a former Jewish neighborhood of old New York. I lived in Philly all my life. I'm a true Philly girl. Everything about me is Philadelphia. I fight my cases like a Philly boxer, tough and fierce. I'm a cocky attorney that never folds under the pressure of the government case, but I'm also warm and lovingly humble. I'm a cheese steak lover. During my lunch breaks I head over to Geno's in South Philly for their delicious cheese steaks and I'm a die hard Eagles fan. I'm 5 foot 4 inches tall with long reddish blond hair that used to be curly until I permed it. I have olive skin with a tight body. I'm in great shape from my daily run and visit to the gym. The only weight I can't seem to lose is on my rear end. I've been told by many of my African-American clients that "you got a butt like a sister." It's definitely an attention getter, so I'm proud of my gluteus maximus.

My gray eyes are big and round and my face is thin like Sarah Jessica Parker. Sometimes I've been mistaken for the beautiful star. In my spare time when I'm not practicing law or busy with my accounting business, I spend time with my handsome husband and my two year old son, Kevin. My husband has a lot of time off from his job as a professor at Temple University when school is in summer recess.

Though I was raised in a strict Jewish household I consider myself liberal, thanks to my husband. When I met him I was very conservative. Tattoos, aagh! Rock and roll--couldn't take it. Defense attorney? Out of the question. My husband was also a student at Harvard law school where I met him. He was raised by liberal parents who attended church only on holidays and funerals. They are Catholic. My husband was a hippie turned career minded academic. Opposites attract. He has tattoos on his back, he listens to rock and roll, and he was once a public defender. He made me loosen up when we started hanging out together amongst our friends. His liberal wisdom also opened my mind to different views of the world. "The world is balanced. That's the way it's always going to be. That's how God wants it. So why wouldn't you be balanced in your judgment of the world. Plus conservative is another way of saying racist, stuck up, soulless and scared to live," he says.

So you're probably wondering how did I end up representing Nafiys Muhammad. Again I have my husband to thank.

XXXXXXXXXXXXXXXXXXXXXXXXX

West Philadelphia

"I don't know what got into these men these days," Miss Samson said to her sister as both elderly women sat in Miss Samson's row house drinking wine. Since leaving Big Butchie, Miss Samson moved into one of the many row homes she owns on a clean, quiet block in one of West Philly's black middle class neighborhoods called Wynnfield.

"They got diarrhea of da mouth that's what there problem is," Miss Samson's younger sister snapped. She was a short, round, dark skinned grouchy woman. She always complained about everything and everybody. She complained about men she dated who stopped calling or always had excuses of not spending time with her, not realizing her constant complaining is what drove them away.

When Butchie was found dead, she complained, "Why did they let a person they know people wanna kill, drop out of protection? The sorry bastards don't care about no black folk any how." Miss Samson sipped her wine out of a champagne glass and continued. "I can't believe this boy done took after his father and snitched on Nafiys. He ain't been nothing but good to these scallies round here. That boy Nafiys, he's a sneaky dangerous guy. He too quiet."

Miss Samson rolled her eyes and shook her head at her sister's complaining. "Quiet is the best way to be. You talk too much, these people going to rat you out." Miss Samson stared at her clock that hung over the kitchen window for a few seconds. "I'm not going to stand by and let these people railroad that boy. His lawyer done stepped off on him cause my sorry ass son made up some crazy story."

Miss Samson removed her cell phone from her black purse and dialed.

"Hello Mister Weinstein. This is Beverly Samson." She smiled while she listened to the man talk. "Yes I've been fine, everybody's ok. Yeah, I'm sorry he had to die that way also. Listen, I have something very important I need to talk to you about. Can I meet you at the school? Tomorrow morning will be fine."

On schedule, Beverly parked her '06 black 4 door Caddy and met Mister Weinstein in one of his empty classrooms. He sat at his desk wearing wire frame spectacles, a brown wool blazer over a black button up shirt. He wore his hair in a pony tail, a reminder of his days looking like a hippie. He looked like the 31 year old version of Steven Seagal. His dark hair and piercing blue eyes made him sinisterly handsome.

Beverly explained her urgency in talking to him. "He needs a lawyer who's not caught up in Philadelphia politics, someone who doesn't grease palms then jerk off using the same grease."

"Beverly, I can't take on the feds. I was a public defender for crying out loud." Beverly laughed while playfully hitting Weinstein's shoulder. She remembered when Weinstein first came out of law school. He pissed a lot of people off in the D.A.'s office and at city hall. He wasn't your average public defender. He actually fought hard for his clients and didn't try to get them to take plea bargains for cases he new the cops didn't have any evidence on. He wasn't the D.A.'s puppet. Beverly heard about him through her colleagues at the law firm she once worked for as a corporate lawyer and her associates in the political circles of city government.

What made Weinstein's story more interesting was that he had a wife with the same guts and drive as he. The difference between the two was the wife didn't go to the public defender office. She started her own practice with money she got from her parents. With the same determination as her husband, she took cases pro-bono and won them all. She didn't bend for anyone. She made D.A's scared and judges edgy. She took nothing personal. If you had the money and she had the time, she took the case and fought it hard.

"I want you to talk to your wife for me. I'll pay whatever it is she wants. I need her to represent Nafiys Muhammad. No lawyer in Philly wants the case because of the Shabazz thing."

Two days after the meeting with Mister Weinstein, Sandra called Beverly. "Mrs. Samson this is Sandra Weinstein. My price is $50,000."

Beverly smiled. "Cash or check?"

XXXXXXXXXXXXXXXXXXXXXXXXXXXX

That is how I wound up with the case. My husband told me about Beverly's plea. I admired the fact that she would pay for the defense of a man that her own son helped the government build a case against because she believed her son was a liar out to save his own ass at the expense of someone who was supposed to be a friend. Plus my husband said." I never liked that Shabazz guy; he's a show boat and a hypocrite to his own religion."

I've had to admit, this is one of the toughest cases I ever had. According to a statement by Shabazz it was Nafiys Muhammad who helped get his daughter back. The thing is, how did he do it and how did he know who to go to? The only people who could answer that are the kidnappers and the people involved. It's Nafiys' word against LiL Butchie's. But it's also his word against Beef whose statement is that LiL Butchies gave him the job of killing his own father with the help of Trisha Parker. LiL Butchie implicates himself in the plot and implicates Nafiys as being his co-plotter. The motive: Big Butchie tried to set them up for the government. A fact documented.

The feds have plenty of photographs of Nafiys and LiL Butchie together. They were the best of friends since childhood. The only time those two have been separated for a while is when Nafiys served ten years for his armored truck conviction. When Nafiys was released from Lewisburg it was LiL Butchie who picked him up from the prison parking lot. The feds were there taking photographs.

Chapter 25

<u>LiL Butchie</u>

Ya'll can say what ya'll want about me, I don't give a fuck. Yeah I played myself. I played myself fucking with that no good bitch Trish. I should've known they would be trailing her dumb ass. Her cell phone got that GPS feature and they caught me coming out of the airport. Then this faggot Beef gon' breakdown and start yapping his gums. And the worst of it is this dude Chris. What made him bring up some shit that happen dam near 30 years ago? What did that have to do with what he got locked up for? Nothing, they stacked the deck on me, man. I know Trish can't hold water and then the F.B.I tells me Nafiys put a hit on me cause the Bilal thing. It's like I had no choice. Go to jail forever or get out in ten? I believe nothing last forever so jail ain't something I'ma start believing does. I choose the ten. All I have to do is testify against Nafiys and plead guilty to obstruction of justice. How did I obstruct justice you ask? Charm money and a gun can go along way in life.

XXXXXXXXXXXXXXXXXXXXXXXXXXXXX

Metropolitan Correction Center

<u>New York 2005</u>

Nafiys sat in the attorney visiting room reading a file that Shabazz handed to him.

"Seems like a pretty fair bunch, Nafiys. I mean fair for what we had to pick from. That's how these federal juries are, they're not all from the inner city. These districts cover the city and the surrounding suburbs so you get a lot of white suburban Jurors. Ya see a lot of these Jurors are from Long Island and upper class sections of Long Island too. Then you got people from nice sections of the city that are scared of the poor parts of the city. Places they read about in their morning paper. "Shabazz said."

Nafiys nodded his head as he looked over the list of names. After the visit, Nafiys with a copy of the list returned to his cell block. Unless a Judge orders for Jurors names and addresses to remain anonymous, the Defense along with the prosecution are given the list of names and addresses of Jurors. The Jury in Nafiys' case weren't sequestered either. They were allowed to return home every night after court.

Nafiys focused his sights on one particular Juror out of the list of 12 and 3 alternates. Nafiys was banking on the fact that the Juror was a black man from the inner city. Nafiys notice that the juror was form the East New York section of Brooklyn. A section Nafiys knew was as rough and reputable as his West Philly neighborhood. Nafiys figured a black man from the ghetto would understand how things are on the streets. He would understand that the U.S government was hell bent on locking almost every black man up, especially ones with money, intellect and influence. That's a threat to the white supremacist fabric of the country. But if the black man didn't have an open mind then... As the barrel chested black man got out of his 99 green Toyota Camry at a gas station on Pennsylvania avenue and Linden boulevard a block away from his Brooklyn home, a sand colored 4 door Nissan Maxima with dark tints pulled up behind the Camry. The Maxima's sound system was at its maximum volume with the sound of the rapper Styles P voice roaring after the chorus blares "I get high, high, high, high giiiigh!"

LiL Butchie got out of the Maxima and approached the barrel chested black man who was a foot taller than LiL Butchie closed in.

"Excuse me, sir. Your name is Matthew Farrow, Right?" Butchie had a piece of paper he was reading off in one hand and the other in the upper pocket of his tan colored Wool rich coat. Matthew Farrow looked confused. He never saw Butchie in his life and was wondering how the thuggish looking man knew his name.

"Yes, that's me. Who are you?" Matthew Farrow asked.

Butchie sensed Farrow on the defensive as if Matthew was ready to strike if necessary.

"My name isn't important. What's important is the safety of yourself and your family," Butchie said calmly removing a thick wad of cash from his pocket. Matthew Farrow stopped pumping gas and faced Butchie aggressively.

"What's that suppose to mean, punk?"
Butchie backed up a little while putting his hand back in his pocket letting it reemerge with a silencer equipped black .40 caliber automatic pistol, making Farrow back up with his hands raised.

"What it means is take the money or this bullet. The bullet is for a guilty verdict and the money is for a not guilty verdict. And your son that attends Gershwin Junior high gets to go to high school. The wife, she gets to continue doing hair at the salon in crown heights. You understand?"

Matthew Farrow understood.

LiL Butchie's mistake was bringing his cousin Beef with him to take care of the Matthew Farrow situation. Beef spilled his guts about it when he was arrested in Vegas. The statement caused the government to arrest Matthew Farrow on his way to work one morning. Matthew Farrow confirmed Beef's story. The feds released Farrow. They understood he was scared for the life of his family.

XXXXXXXXXXXXXXXXXXXXXXXX

I gave Nafiys the opportunity to spend time with his family by getting to that juror dude. If it wasn't for me that nigga would be doing a thousand years added to a life sentence. He knows them J.B.M niggas would've killed me if I didn't set Bilal up. Again the choice, me or Bilal. Who else would I choose? He could've at least shown me more respect and put more than ten thousand on my head. Dam I'm only worth 8 stacks dead?

Chapter 26

<u>Charles Heinz, Assistant U.S. Attorney</u>

9:00 A.M
Federal Courthouse
<u>Philadelphia:</u>

In order for you to fully understand this case Ladies and gentlemen of the jury, you must first understand the defendant, Mr. Nafiys Muhammad, the man sitting at the defense table wearing a black suit, white shirt and yellow tie. You must also understand the other individuals involved in this case. Individuals who participated in the crimes charged in the indictment. Individuals who will testify that they actively participated in a murder for hire and a kidnapping, they will testify that it was the defendant Nafiys Muhammad who hired and ordered the murder of Butch Samson and the kidnapping of a little girl name Khadijah Shabazz.

You will hear testimony about motive. The motive the defendant had to kidnap Khadijah and motive to order the killing of Butch Samson. These individuals you will hear testimony from are criminals, bad criminals who have committed heinous crimes. Ladies and gentlemen, I submit to you that criminals are usually and most likely the ones involved with other criminals who are in the same pursuit of greed and deception in order to further the activities of the gang or group. This is what this case is about. It's about Nafiys Muhammad. Kidnapping the daughter of a prominent Philly attorney, acting as if he saved the daughter of the attorney, so that this attorney would represent Mr.

Muhammad and his cohorts for a lower price, or in some cases free of charge. It's total deception ladies and gentlemen, cold hearted deception. You will hear from the man who kidnapped the girl. He will testify about why the Kidnapping took place, who master minded it and how it ended.

The same man will testify of why Butch Samson was killed. This man is Butch's son known on the streets as Little Butch. A man who aided in planning the murder of his father with the defendant Nafiys Muhammad. Little Butch Samson will also testify about the trafficking of drugs from New York and Philadelphia.

Ladies and Gentlemen of the Jury, after you hear the testimony of the many witnesses, some I mentioned, some I haven't, you will undoubtedly, following the instructions of law that you are to apply to the evidence, return a verdict of guilty on all charges against the defendant, Mr. Nafiys Muhammad. Thank you.

XXXXXXXXXXXXXXXXXXXXXXXXXXX

I listened to Mrs. Weinstein's opening argument, which lasted almost an hour. I watched the face of the jurors as Mrs. Weinstein made a heart felt, slightly convincing argument in defense of Mr. Muhammad. I couldn't read their faces and tell if the argument she put up made mine seem like a bunch of unsupported rhetoric. Juries are mysterious like that at times.

"The witnesses the government will call are witnesses who claimed to have personal knowledge and an active role in crimes that happened a while back, only to come forth with the information when they themselves were arrested for very serious crimes. Crimes that would put them away forever or possibly receive a sentence of death. So they make up stories that will save them from these severe punishments and the government awards them with lighter sentences.

I find it kind of strange that the government would plea bargain with the actual killer to put a person they felt help plan the killing away longer than the murderer. What kind of message is this government sending to the American people?"

After listening to Mrs. Weinstein's argument, the judge ordered a recess. I immediately went to my office, a block away from the courthouse, after being summoned by the U.S Attorney for the Eastern District of Pennsylvania, my boss. When I got to the office, I saw the U.S attorney's usual tanned face looking pale and sullen.

"Good afternoon, sir. How may I be of assistance?" I asked cordially.

"There's been a setback in your case," the U.S attorney murmured as if he were on the verge of telling me someone in my family passed away.

"The Classon guy is missing," he continued.
If things couldn't get any worst. "For god's sake how does a person in witness protection go missing and cant be found!" I pondered angrily.

"Apparently he went on vacation to Arizona. The Arizona authorities are on it now. There is an APB out on him as we speak." The U.S attorney said, as if the APB would help me. I go back in the courtroom in less than a half hour with one of my witnesses missing. A critical witness.

"Don't let it stop you, Charles. You still have witnesses that can help put Muhammad away for life."

Yeah witnesses that the defense already hammered their already shattered credibility. Classon is the most articulate and solid witness we have. Little Butchie had a prior statement where he claimed responsibility for his own involvement in the distribution and sale of drugs that the government alleged belong to Muhammad.

This Beef guy never discussed the murder plot of Big Butch with Muhammad, he only had direct contact with Little Butchie, and the same goes for Trish Parker. How do I make these witnesses believable when they're actually equally dangerous to Muhammad? In fact, Muhammad could be made to look less dangerous with his propensity to stand clear of the dirty work while running legitimate businesses.

This is going to be a rough one.

"I won't let it stop me, sir."

Chapter 27

<u>Nasir Shabazz</u>

After testifying about that September morning, my daughter was kidnapped, I sat with my wife in the spectators section only once looking at Nafiys. I had to point to him when the U.S attorney asked me to identify the defendant. Nafiys had the audacity to look at me as if he was disappointed in me.

Me, my wife and other family and friends sat behind the prosecution side of the courtroom. Most of the people that came to court to support us were members of the masjid we attended in Germantown. People who used to look at Nafiys as their Muslim brother. People me and him gave jobs to and enjoyed social gatherings with. People who trusted him around their loved ones, particularly children. Nafiys and I sponsored and financed trips to amusement parks, family outing and other event. They all felt betrayed by Nafiys.

After calling me as a witness, the government called my now 14 year old daughter Khadijah to testify.

"Can you state your name for the record?"

"Khadijah Shabazz." Her voice sounded shaky and child like.

In full female Muslim attire, Khadijah boldly sat there facing Nafiys. A man she called "Uncle Fiys." A man whom when she saw him lit up, running to embrace him. A man she would defend when other kids would taunt her with harsh words about her infamous uncle. "He is a drug dealing Muslim............" "My mom said your uncle is a killer......." "He kills Muslim too"......." "Why does your father be his Lawyer. Your father likes Killers?"

Khadijah would yell that they were wrong and sometimes get into fights causing me or my wife to have to go to her school to straighten her out. I hate to have to have her in this courtroom reliving a chapter in her life she wanted out of her memory, only to find out that the man she adored masterminded that terrible event.

"Khadijah, do you remember September 4 1995, that particular morning?"

Khadijah leaned her small lips close to the microphone and focused her big brown eyes to the jury.

"Yes I do."

"Can you tell members of this jury what happened?"

XXXXXXXXXXXXXXXXXXXXXXXX

1995, Philly

"I don't know AKI (brothers) I owe a lot to that brother."

"No one gets hurt in the deal. He's the best lawyer in Philly. We need him in our grip. He'll be like our Bruce Cutler." Abdul Latif, Shabazz's friend and neighbor nodded his head reluctantly as a line backer sized brother in a black Dickie suit, tan Timberlands and a white Kufi on his head relayed a plan that involved the kidnapping of his friend and one time attorney's daughter.

A child Abdul Latif treated as his own. A child that attended the school he taught karate at. A child he was entrusted to bring to school along with his daughter. A baby who's diaper he changed while he babysat or his wife babysat when the Shabazz were out.

After saying the greetings to her father, little Khadijah crossed the street on the quiet block after looking both ways as she was taught. She knocked on Abdul Latif's wooden door after opening the screen door. No one answered. After a few more knocks, Khadijah walked down the stairs headed back towards her home. A light skinned man emerged from a parked car in front of Abdul Latif's home. The man wore a close crop beard, a black leather jacket, black jeans and a black pair of Timberland Chukkas. Khadijah looked at him shortly then continued to walk. Suddenly, she felt a hand over her mouth and a strong grip around her body.

She couldn't scream and the man was too strong for her to break loose. She kicked frantically while being carried to the back of a brown four-door sedan. Khadijah watched as the back door open and the man shoved her in the back next to another man who looked dangerously handsome. He wore his black ski hat halfway off his curly hair and played with a tooth pick he had in the corner of his mouth.

"You scream, you die little girl. Then we kill your mom and dad," the man with the toothpick said, as another man in the driver's seat drove off. Unexpectedly, Khadijah remained calm in the backseat though she was scared to death. Her small heart beat rapidly and she had thoughts of never seeing her mom and dad again.

The kidnappers drove her into the dirty, grimy streets of North Philadelphia. They parked in front of a house on a small block. The house was the only house on the block that looked occupied or livable. The other row homes were boarded up or gutted. The block was littered with broken glass, syringes, garbage and graffiti. The same man who adducted Khadijah carried her in his arms like she was his child into the row home.

The dingy exterior of the house was the total opposite of the interior. The home was nicely furnished. Tan leather couches sat in the living room surrounding a state of the art entertainment system. A 50 inch television took up a large part of the living room.

Raekwon's "Only built for Cuban links" blasted from the system as Khadijah sat on the couch. The curly haired, dangerous looking guy came in the room with a cordless phone and sat next to Khadijah. Then the guy who abducted her pointed to the play station while smiling at Khadijah. "You wanna play?" Khadijah shook her head in the negative.

The guy shrugged his shoulders. "Just tryna be nice."

Khadijah stared at the guy on the cordless phone as he motioned for the play station guy to turn the music down. Khadijah knew she would always remember his face. Then she heard the curly head guy say into the phone:

"We got your daughter. Bring a hunnit grand to Connie Mack Park."

Khadijah was allowed to speak to her father. Hearing her father's voice brought out the emotions she had built up since she was abducted.

"Daddy, I wanna come home!" Khadijah cried.

Shabazz assured his daughter everything was going to be alright even though he was unsure if he would ever see his daughter again alive.

The men fed Khadijah McDonalds happy meal, which she picked at and barely ate. She lost her appetite. After the phone call, she cried most of the day. She fell asleep and was awakened the next morning by the curly haired man.

"Cmon youngn, it's time for you to go home."

Khadijah wiped her eyes and followed the man out to the same car they arrived in. She noticed it was still dark outside and the cold air woke her completely up. They drove a block away from the house and parked behind a car whose break lights were lit up. The back door of the car opened up. Khadijah was led out of the ca and into a green Mercedes Benz 500.

A man stuck his head out of the backseat smiling at Khadijah.

"As Salaamu Alaiykum Khadijah," the man said.

Khadijah cried while mumbling," Wa alaiykum Salaam. I wanna go home." "You are now," The man said. Then his door closed.

Khadijah was walked another block up entering Connie Mack park. Where she was met by Abdul Latif. At the sight of Abdul Latif she cried and ran to him. "Uncle Latif!"

"Khadijah, are you alright. It's Ok baby, I'm here. And your Abu is coming to get you."

A few minutes, later Shabazz showed up to get his daughter.

XXXXXXXXXXXXXXXXXXXXXXXX

Back in Court

"Khadijah, I'm going to show you a picture of a man. I want you to tell the jury if you recognize him and from where." The U.S attorney said with a photo in hand.

"That's one of the men who kidnapped me." Khadijah answered. The U.S attorney too the photo and showed it to the jury.

"Your honor, let the record reflect that the witness has identified Butch "Little Butch" Samson as one of her kidnappers.

I knew from the time I laid eyes on that guy that he was no good. A point I stressed to Nafiys plenty of times. Little Butch is weak. He isn't cut out for the life he is tryna live. I was right about him, but wrong about Nafiys.

"I have no further questions your honor."

Chapter 28

<u>Chris</u>

I remember I lived in West Philly around the time Bilal and his crew were making a name for themselves. In fact as a youngster I ran errands for Bilal at only 8 years old. My grandmother lived in West Philly and I spent a lot of time at the home. When I turned 12 I moved back to my mom's house in North Philly. I still visited West Philly every summer. I looked up to Bilal back then, he was a Hustla's hustla. I had to stay away from West Philly after a while. When I turned 13 I shot a guy trying to rob my cousin. The robber was a member of Bilal's crew. The shooting worked in my favor in another way. It gave me a rep. A baw who wouldn't hesitate to pull the trigger.

So you're probably saying your reputation means nothing now cause I'm testifying for the feds. Hey I gotta do what I gotta do. It's easy for people to judge until they get in situations like this. I know plenty of dudes who stood on corners with their homeys talking all that stand up, never folding under pressure shit, but when the feds pop up with those indictments, all of a sudden they start singing a different tune and on the stand pointing fingers.

Ain't nobody loyal on them streets these days. It ain't part of the game no more. It's every man for themselves out there. Look at LiL Butchie. He helped set up his man's older brother. And for what? Fear, if you're scared, you shouldn't be in the game. Then he tells Nafiys that Bilal got killed at a dice game by some young Baw that Bilal watched grow up. He even went as far as to make up who did it.

"Yo, LiL Poo did that shit for them J.B.M cats," LiL Butchie told Nafiys over the phone while Nafiys was locked up. Sadly that same week LiL Poo was killed cause of Butchie's lie. There were a lot of rumors of what happen to Bilal. One thing for sure, the J.B. M was behind it. Bilal was making too much money.

I guess the government wants me to testify about the Bilal setup to show Nafiys' motive in being LiL Butchie's enemy. LiL Butchie has a hit on his head, according to Shabazz. Shabazz testified that he informed Nafiys about my statement to the police. A seven-page statement that read like an urban novel.

"You gave a graphic statement to the authorities concerning a war on the streets of Philadelphia. Can you tell this jury what year the war started and the cause of the war?" The U.S attorney asked me. This was a part of the statement Shabazz didn't get to see.

XXXXXXXXXXXXXXXXXXXXXXXX

Philadelphia 1992

"Yo, my cousin is home, Chris." My homey Speedy told me as we rolled up a blunt of dust we just copped off of 7th and Pike. Speedy drove us in his 91 Cream colored Acura Legend with cream BBS rims. I knew Speedy was related to Bilal and Nafiys. What Speedy didn't know was that I was responsible for his cousin's death. Honestly, I don't think he would even care if he found out. For some reason he had a lot of animosity towards his blood relations.

Ever since Speedy and the guys he caught the armored truck robbery case with, including Nafiys, He distanced himself from his West Philly family and neighborhood. There were rumors that Speedy told the cops on the crew but everyone knew them dudes got caught red-handed, so he didn't have to tell. Plus they all pled guilty. The rumor spread because Speedy is the only one that was on the streets while the rest stayed in jail. I never saw paperwork so I couldn't say that the baw was a rat with no proof. Speedy is a good dude. He helped me make a lot of money. He sold a lot of coke in Germantown and put me on the customers who bought a lot of weight so I could rob them.

"What's he up to?" I asked concerning Speedy's revelation of Nafiys' release from the pen.

"I don't know, but that nigga threw dirt on my name and he gon' pay for that," Speedy said with tight jaws. I saw the muscles of his jaw flex as he spoke.

"Listen homey, I got you. I know somebody that could get that nigga somewhere we can get him," I shared with Speedy. I wasn't gonna tell him how or who I would use. That's too much info for him.

"How?" Speedy asked curiously.

"Do you want me to do it?" I asked wanting to leave the details out.

"Yeah but how?" Speedy asked again.

"I'll show you betta than I can tell you."

Two days later, I met up with the person I knew could make Nafiys' demise come early and easy. We met up at a club called Gotham on Delaware avenue. We both were dressed in V.I.P style. Of course in the V.I.P section. LiL Butchie wore a canary yellow linen button up. White linen pants and white ostrich skin shoes. The canary yellow diamond pinky ring matched the shirt and the bezel of his watch. His curly hair was lined up Steve Harvey sharp.

I wore a sky blue button up by Polo, spectacles by Polo, black Polo slacks and black gator shoes with a gold buckle. We drank Dom Perignon sitting on a couch in the V.I.P section. LiL Butchie's eyes widened at my request.

"Why him?" LiL Butchie asked.

"The same reason his brother got it. He can get in the way," I replied. LiL Butchie looked at me as if he were waiting for me to tell him I was just joking. I guess the look on my face made him realize I was dead serious.

"He ain't in the game no more. That's the truth." LiL Butchie shot back. I couldn't come up with an excuse better than the one I already tried to use. So I kept it official with Butchie. Plus I figured I could get more insight on Speedy's motive.

"It's for Speedy. Speedy said Nafiys threw dirt on his name. He wants some pay back."

"Speedy! You talking bout rat ass Speedy?" Butchie roared.

"Why niggas saying that. Didn't all them niggas cop out?" I enquire.

"Yeah that's cause Speedy's the one that had the cops waiting for them. He caught a case and the feds picked it up. He was tryna get my pops and them locked up on some drug jawn. The truck robbery came up and he gave them that. Chris I seen the paperwork," Butchie relayed convincingly.

I guess after me and Butchie's conversation, Butchie informed Nafiys about Speedy's intentions. Speedy one night called me frantically while I was sexing this thick chocolate chick.

"Chris, yo niggas shot my car up. It was some West Philly niggas. I know my cousin behind it!

"Yo, calm down nigga. Where you at?" I asked while the chocolate honey continued to go down on me. I laid on my back and held her head as she took all of me in her mouth.

"I'm up in Somerville. I jumped out my car and ran to get a hack. Yo it's on nigga. I need some guns. I'm a handle this!"

Out of curiosity I gave Speedy a few guns to see how he would handle the situation. He's never been known as a gunslinger, he's the type that pays well for someone else to do his dirty work. Speedy is a pretty boy. He struts around town in Polo gear from head to toe. He plays the gym a lot, lifting light weights and he runs ball on a regular. So he's in tip top shape. Not bulky but cut and lean. He has brown skin that resembles the tune of an almond. His high cheek bones and oval eyes give him a look of Ethiopian ancestry. And his height is what earned him his moniker. He grew to six feet by the time he was 14 years old. His height going up so quick made his father call him Speedy. Speed wouldn't hurt a fly. Women and basketball were his favorite pastimes. Guns isn't his thing.

I guess Speedy had something to prove. He round up a couple of young wild boys from up Germantown and went to war with a couple of guys from West Philly. At first, Speedy and his gang of 3 young baw scored a few points when they shot up the corner of 54th and market wounding two young cats who were out there hustling. The wounds were non-life threatening but a point was made. Speedy was ready for war. Then things turned bad for the Speedy gang.

One of the 3 young Germantown boys was spotted at club McDonalds on North Philly's diamond street with a pretty Puerto-Rican girl. The Germantown boy leaned on the hood of his black Delta 88 while the Puerto-Rican girl stood in a bowlegged stance in front of him.

"Hey my man, you wouldn't happen to have a light on you?" an older looking guy wearing a Temple University sweatshirt and a gray black stripe Negro League baseball cap asked the Germantown boy. The older guy looked at the young boy's face saying to himself he can't be no more than 17 years of age.

"Yeah I got one," the young boy replied reaching in his dark blue Guess Jeans for the lighter. He pulled the lighter out and lit it using both hands to block the flame from the night breeze coming off of the Schuykill River. The older guy held the cigarette in his mouth while the young boy lit it. With his free hand the older guy placed a black .357 magnum to the young guys chin and squeezed the trigger. Boom!

His head jerked back violently while the top of it popped like a large pimple. His body hit the hood of his car and dropped to the ground. The Puerto-Rican girl screamed as the crowded parking lot turned into a racetrack of frantic people running in different directions, some ducking behind their vehicles trying to see where the gun shots were coming from.

The older guy stopped the Puerto-Rican girl from screaming with a shot to her mouth. The bullet smashed into her teeth shattering them, then travelling to the back of her throat exiting out the back of her neck shattering the brain stem. She was dead before her body hit the ground.

When Speedy found out about the double murder, he was scared shitless. I knew the Puerto-Rican girl's brother. He is a cool dude from the badlands I went to school with. Whenever I needed something like a package of coke or a few bags of the wet, he looked out. So I wanted to pay him back by bringing him a body of at least somebody down with the West Philly crew responsible for the murder of his baby sister. I told him about the whole situation.

"She got caught in the midst Pete. It wasn't for her," I told my Puerto-Rican homey. He didn't care about what I said. He wanted someone to pay. I somewhat understood his reasoning. Me personally, I wanted the trigger man. Still in all, I gave Pete what he wanted.

I told the target to meet me on 7th and Pike where Pete hustled the dust I smoked faithfully. He showed up a half hour after I called him. It was a chilly night and the target wore a Guess leather jacket when he emerged from his red MPV van. He approached me looking around nervously.

"Yo Chris, what's up man. I'm leaving Philly for a while until the heat die down," he said. I stood in front of an abandon row home smoking a Newport.

"Chill out nigga, ain't no heat on you. I gotta show you something I got in my car," I said walking over to a brick red Bonneville with the target behind me. I opened the driver's side passenger door once I got to the Bonneville.

"Check out these gats," I said pointing into the backseat backing away from the door as the target approached. As soon as he looked in the back seat, his eyes widened in shock and fear. Pete laid down on the seat pointing a black Mac 11 at him. Before he could run or scream, the Mac 11 erupted flashing in the back seat. The bullets ripped the target's face and Guess leather apart.

Speedy dropped dead as I walked away and got in my Camry.

XXXXXXXXXXXXXXXXXXXXXXXXXXXX

"Did you ever gain personal knowledge of who was responsible for the death of the young Spanish girl and the young guy from West Philadelphia?" The U.S attorney asked me.

"Personal knowledge? Of course, I have personal knowledge. I've been a hired gun for years in Philly. That man right there hired me."

"Let the record reflect that the witness has pointed to the defendant Nafiys Muhammad," the U.S attorney said with a sly grin on his face.

Nafiys also had a smirk on his face as I pointed at him. I know what the nigga's thinking. Yeah I'm a chump for snitching on his ass. Yeah, well he's a chump cause he's scared to pull the trigger on his own.

(Nafiys' Thoughts)

This nigga's testifying about shit that I'm not even charged with. Why would they bring up those two murders without me being charged, what are these people up to? I guess I have to find out.

Chapter 29

<u>Sandra Weinstein Esquire</u>

I'm allergic to losing. I don't know what it's like to lose a case. I don't even know what its like to be close to losing. I mean I've been unsure at times because Juries are unpredictable, but this case is one where my allergies to losing are flaring. When the government introduced evidence of a double homicide my client wasn't charged with. The Judge ordered me and the U.S attorney into his chambers for a meeting.

"I'm introducing modus operandi, your honor; the defendant's method of dealing with his adversaries. By bringing in the testimony, it's showing the character of the defendant," the U.S attorney said as he and I stood in front of the large Oakwood desk where the Judge sat.

"There's no corroborating evidence to these murders alleged in the witness' testimony. This is prejudicial severely outweighing the probative value. In fact, your honor, this is a surprise. Why wasn't I informed of this through the discovery process? This is clearly a Brady violation." After a few more minutes of arguing legal jargon, the judge made his ruling.

"I disagree with it being a Brady violation. He isn't charged with the murders or conspiracy to commit. Even if he was, the evidence wouldn't be exculpatory. Brady deals with the withholding of evidence that would have been exculpatory and helpful to the Defendant. I also disagree with the modus operand theory, due to the fact of the defendant having no prior background of hired murders.

The testimony goes to motive and character of the defendant, therefore it is allowed."

"This isn't going the way I planned. I guess my record remained impeccable because cases I knew I couldn't win I wouldn't take. I took this case as a favor to my husband. He even helped me prepare for it. I can't say he didn't warn me.

"Honey, I looked over the case. Now you know my theory is that every case is beatable, even the ones where the defendant is dead wrong. You just hate to work the maze and find that way to the end of it. Find the weakness of the case and that's where you dig your way out of the maze. With this case, dig fast, cause if you don't, the rain is going to make the ground muddy and your feet will sink in the mud and get stuck."

Once we're back in the courtroom, I cross examined this Chris guy vigorously. I tried every which way to trip him up but obviously this guy was a raconteur. He was extremely calm and his diction surprised me.

"Maam, you may think I'm lying in favor of the government, but if you did your homework, I was telling the F. B.I and the Philadelphia police about these crimes before a deal was ever struck. I have a conscience contrary to what you may perceive."

He's the type of witness prosecutors have wet dreams about. He showed no signs of nervousness; he didn't trip up in his words. He was unitimidated by a sharp, gun-blazing, defense attorney and he sounded convincing.

Everyday after court I talk to Nafiys about how the case was going. Well most of the time he asked how I thought it was going. And I don't lie to my clients. "Honestly Nafiys, it looks bad."

Getting to know Nafiys, I found him a very likeable person. He is extremely humble and he doesn't react emotionally to situations that affect him negatively. What I like most about him is that, when I tell him it looks bad, he doesn't fly off the handle like a lot of clients usually do.

"Don't worry about it. You're doing a very good job. Whatever happens is supposed to happen."

His response makes me fight harder. My opinion of his guilt or innocence doesn't matter. Everyone deserves a fair trial and a lawyer who makes sure that the client's rights are secured. If things go bad for Nafiys at trial, I had a plan B that I ran by Nafiys for approval.

"Go for It."

Chapter 30

Trish

Federal Detention Center
Philadelphia:

This jail thing is truly not for me. I spend most of my day crying and sleeping. The food is terrible and these women are irritating, some of them at least. I'm in bad need of a manicure, pedicure, a trip to the hair salon and some serious spa treatment. A visit to the Bliss Spa in Sotto would do justice for a sister. A facial coupled with a carrot and sesame body buff with a hot oil massage, umh! Ya'll just don't know.

Today I cried a lot. An F.B.I agent visited me asking me do I know where Class would go when he wants to get away. Or do I know any place or person in Arizona who Class would visit. When I asked why they were asking me these things I had no answer. The agent simply said,
"He's missing."

"So where is my daughter?" I cried. I wouldn't be able to handle hearing she is missing too. What if someone got to Class and Coco was with him. They would kill her along with him.

"She is in custody of the U.S Marshall Service. We have contacted some of her and your relatives in New York. They are willing to take her in."
Thank God! Was all I could think of, hearing that it was Lavelle who took Coco in with a relief. Lavelle would make sure Coco is well taken care of.

There was only one person I could talk to in the jail. The only person I was comfortable talking to. We shared a lot of the same taste in style as far as clothing and accessories. We were both New Yorkers, she, from Brooklyn and me Harlem, and we loved money. Sadly for me and wonderful for her was the fact that she was leaving and headed back to the streets.

She was stronger in spirit than me; she was extremely smart and listened attentively as I cried on her shoulder. I wish I knew her before this experience. I probably would've made better choices. She's much prettier and shorter in person. I got a lotta love for this little female rapper.

One thing I gained most for her besides the love was respect. She stood strong when all her so called friends turned on her. She is loyal as hell. I wish I had that quality about me. Even when she came to me one day as I sat in the dayroom watching General Hospital on the block T.V and said:

"Trish, why didn't you tell me you were a government witness?" I didn't know there was a rule that said I had to share my business with her or anybody to say the least. And her tone was a little on the aggressive side. I still had respect for her.

"You didn't ask me. Why, what's up?" I asked slightly on the defensive and a little confused and curious to why she was asking.

"I don't condone that Trish. It's the reason I'm in here," she said standing over me with her little arms folded across her chest. The orange jumpsuit couldn't conceal the big breasts she totes.

"You're not facing forever away from your daughter. You're not looking at life in the shit hole cause some grimy niggas put your name in some murder and kidnapping shit. Niggas told on me, so whoever told you my business, tell them to tell the whole story!" I said angrily and walked to my cell.

I don't care what those broke down broads think. Them bitches couldn't walk in my socks, let alone my shoes. Most of them would've done the same shit in my situation. I bet you my life the majority of them are snitches tryna front.

She stopped talking to me after that conversation. I wish she wouldn't though. My days weren't the same without her to talk to. You can talk to her about anything and she is wise enough to elaborate on with wisdom. She had a lot of mail to read so sometimes her day would be occupied with that task. But she would always find time to tale to me.

When she left, things on the block were dull. She was the soul of our small cell block. Before she was released, she stopped by my cell.

"Trish, you be safe, ma. Do what your heart tells you is right. In the long run you'll be able to live with your decision, if it's the right one."

That was the last thing she said to me before departing. I'm not too much of a Hip Hop fan but since meeting her I listen to her music every time I hear it. That girl is the shit. I understood her advice to me and I truly respect it. So it was a shock to everyone when I walked in the cherry paneled courtroom after I was called to take the stand, looking at the people in the spectators section, people I never saw before giving me dirty looks, while some men stared in awe at my voluptuous shape shown under the Burberry skirt and blouse. I started into the microphone, "I lied to the F.B.I about this whole thing. My statement is a lie. Butchie is lying about Nafiys having anything to do with this."

Of course, the U.S attorney scowled at me while the Judge threatened.

"Miss Parker, you're under oath."

"I know. This is why I'm telling the truth. I lied for a deal just like Butchie is doing. He don't work for Nafiys. He works for himself. When I got off the stand, the U.S attorneys face was beet red as was the F.B.I agents who watched. I looked over at the table where Nafiys and his lawyer sat. Nafiys didn't look at me and his lawyer had a smile on her face. Of course, I was charged with making a false statement, but so what. I can live with it. I have a petite rapper that I met in jail to thank for that. I love you, Uncle Bish.

Chapter 31

Sherry Anderson

The Conclusion:

Wow! I thought while sitting in the back of the courtroom listening to Trish Parker flush the government case down the toilet. This is the last task I've taken to complete the story on the history and story of the Black Top Crew. If Nafiys beats this case, I'll probably do another issue about this crew. Hopefully I won't have to interview or attempt to interview Nafiys or any of his comrades behind prison walls.

I must say that was definitely a bold move that Trish made. I guess her conscience got the best of her and she decided to take responsibility for her own actions. Hopefully the valuable lesson she gained by all of this is to be cautious of the people, place and things you put yourself around. Living in the moment won't prepare you for the long run. Life is unpredictable, death is predictable.

I chose not to write or record my interview with Tank or his son Class. Class didn't have too much to say while we sat on the hot patio in Arizona. All he talked about is tryna get a date with me. Of course I acted as if I would take up his offer cause I had an ulterior motive.

XXXXXXXXXXXXXXXXXXXXXXXXX

Arizona:

"It's no secret that you have a girl. It was all in the paper in New York when your house got raided in Long

Island. Your woman, the mother of your child was there." I half smiled telling Class as we sat on the patio waiting for Tank to return from inside the house. Class was putting all of his charm into action as he stared me in my eyes. The plastic surgery they did on him was professional. You couldn't tell that his face was altered. No Michael Jackson affect, no tight, plastic face look; it looked natural.

When there was a god sent breeze within the scorching Arizona day, I could smell the Issi, Miyaki cologne he wore.

"Those days are over. I found out a lot about this chick that could be a smash at the box office if the story became a movie," Class said.

That's a hell of an idea. I could write a true crime novel about the Black Top Crew and sell the movie rights. I could even write a fiction novel based on the crew.

"If we were to go on a date, where would you take me?" I asked Class with a flirtatious smile. I could see the excitement in his face after my act of interest.

"I can throw down on the stove, so I would take you on a picnic…maybe on a beach in the Bahamas."

"Sounds good. Let's start with the movie right now."

"Let's do this," Class said quickly. Tank returned from inside the house. Class informed him of me and his date to the movies and that he would return that night.

"It was a pleasure meeting you Tank. Thank you for your time. I enjoyed your company." I shook Tank's gorilla size hand.

Me and Class both drove in our rented cars to a movie theater in Downtown Phoenix. It was a matinee so the theater was empty. Me, him and another couple sat in the theater watching "The Devil wears Prada." We sat in the back and like a typical man he paid more attention to trying to slide his hand up my skirt than watching the movie. I pushed his hand away and whispered, "I'm on my period." I unzipped his slacks and removed his swollen organ. Another Wow! I held what felt like an elephant's trunk in my hand and slowly stroked it. I could hear Class moan a little as I moved my hand softly up and down his shaft.

"I have to use the bathroom Class. Keep it stiff for me," I whispered in his ear seductively. He placed his pole back in his pants.

"Don't take too long, baby girl," he mumbled.

I got up and walked out of the dark auditorium. Class sat there staring at the back of the other couples head until they got up and begin walking towards the exit. When they got close, Class noticed the couples were both men. Class looked away after mumbling, "Faggots" to himself.

In a split second, Class felt something smash into his head then he saw darkness. About a half hour later, a dizzy and disoriented Class laid in the back of a black Econoline van. He felt the cold metal of the van floor against his face as his vision cleared. Then he felt a gloved hand smacking his face.

"Hey brother, wake up, homey!" a voice unfamiliar to Class said in a deep voice. Class lift his head up now realizing his hands were tied behind his back and his ankles tied to the rope on his wrist. He was hog tied and duct taped around his mouth. Class looked at the man sitting on the tire hump in front of him. No recognition.

"Damn, I finally get to meet you, homey," the man said with a grin on his dark complexioned face. Class could tell that the black bucket hat sat on a low hair cut. The brim of the hat concealed half of the man's eyes. Class then noticed the silver 50 cal Desert Eagle on the guy's jacket that sat on the floor beside him.

"Baby, we're here," Class heard the familiar voice of mine coming from the driver's seat. I know if he could he would kick himself in the ass for letting his guard down. I know I would if I was in his position.

Class mumbled under the duct tape. The man ripped the tape off his mouth. "Sherry, why are you doing this, who sent you?" Class roared. The man picked the gun up and smacked Class on the head with it.

"Nigga, shut up and watch how you talk to my wife!"

I stopped the van in a deserted area of the the Arizona desert. The man with me, my husband got out the back of the van, pulling Class' tied up body with him. I came from around the van and saw the hole my husband dug for Class' body. Class saw it too.

"Hey yo, man, please don't kill me. I got paper, homey, millions stashed. I'll get it to you A.S.A.P. Yo, please don't kill me!" Class begged and cried. He sounded nothing like the charming Mack he was when he tried to seduce me. This wasn't the guy on the witness stand testifying on his own brother and Nafiys as if he were telling a war story to a homey. No, this guy sounds like a baby screaming for his mommy.

My husband laughed. "Damn player, at least die like a man."

"I don't wanna die man, please yo. Whatever you want man, I'll get it. I swear on my moms. I swear on my daughter!" Class cried.

"You don't have a daughter. We know the kid ain't yours," I teased. Me and my husband laughed at my joke.

"Hey guess what Class. You know who I am, man?" My husband asked.

"Na man. If Nafiys sent you, tell him I'm sorry, man. I'll take it back, man. I'll sign an affidavit!" Me and my husband looked at each other as if to say yeah right.

"I have nothing to do with Nafiys, brother. Betta yet little brother," my husband said.

Class looked at him with bug eyes. "You're Keenan Junior?"

"Is that your final answer?" my husband joked.

"Listen Keenan, why you doing this?"

My husband held his chin as if he were in deep thought. He then looked me in my eyes. "Let me see. You're a rat who sold out his own family. You and that old rat of a father making the family look bad. Somebody has to make some corrections. Someone has to purify the blood line."

The night desert air was a little cold and I wanted for this charade to end. I put in a lot of time to find out where Class and Tank were, and to put this plan in motion. I wanted to get back home and back to the business of running the magazine, which me and my husband, Mr. and Mrs. Keenan and Stephanie Giles owned.

"I don't want yo money, nigga. I wanna burry you alive like you did our brother Corey," Keenan barked. Keenan dragged Class' body to the rim of the six food hole in the hard desert terrain. With one timberland booted foot. Keenan kicked Class in the hole. Class screamed, "Please man, don't do this!" And my husband grabbed shovels from the back of the van and buried Class alive.

Meanwhile the plan to kill Tank was more difficult due to the level of security Tank had around his fortress of a house. But we came up with the best way to rid the world of Keenan "Tank" Giles. We attached a bomb that would level the house to Class' rental car. As Tank sat on his porch, he watched in shock as a speeding car crashed through his gate and came to a stop in front of his patio only to explode. The explosion could be seen in Phoenix. The house almost disintegrated from the explosion. Tank's dismembered body was found half way up the block. All the gadgets and security equipment helped the bomb create more damage. The wiring that ran through and under the house was fuel for the C-4. It was over for him.

My husband and I drove out of the desert headed to the airport to catch a flight back to New York

XXXXXXXXXXXXXXXXXXXXXXXXXXXXX

If Class would've testified at Nafiys trial and Trish didn't renege, the U.S attorney's closing argument would have been tight, but his case got pretty much destroyed with Trish's unexpected revelation. The government didn't have too much to work with, but Nafiys' lawyer brought it home when she gave her sermon-like closing statement.

"You heard the government's witnesses. You were able to see their demeanors. You heard their self serving tales against my client in order to get a slap on the wrist for heinous acts they've committed, not Mr. Muhammad. Even without Ms. Parker telling you that Little Butchie lied. Little Butchie himself showed how much of a liar he is. He wrote a statement to the F.B.I in 2005 saying that he never worked for my client in the drug business. He was supplied by his dope dealing father. He didn't receive anything from my client.

The guy who calls himself Beef never mentioned my client being involved in the conspiracy to kill Butch Samson. And who was the other kidnapper of Khadijah Shabazz besides Little Butchie? Why didn't Little Butchie say who he was? Why doesn't the government tell us who he is? What is little Butchie and the government hiding? I'll tell you what they're hiding. They are hiding behind Little Butchie's lies.

Where is this New York Connection they mentioned?"

That was a low blow from Nafiys' lawyer. She knew that Class was missing.   But hey why not expose the government. Bring it home baby!

Then the lawyer continued to hammer at the government's case with:

"There is no New York connection ladies and gentlemen. It's a myth, a fishing expedition. My client has a wife who lives in New York, an honest hard working woman. Is that the New York connection? Or is it more sinister than that? My client is a legitimate business owner who employs people of his faith. He is a Muslim and they don't like Muslims, the F.B.I

"Objection your honor counselor is out of line and this is beyond the scope of a closing argument. It is highly prejudicial and misleading!" the U.S attorney yelled.

"Counselor, I will not allow that in my courtroom. Objection sustained," the judge said to the lawyer of Nafiys. He looked at the jury and advised: "The counselor's comment about religious bias is unwarranted and should be disregarded from the record." The lawyer continued.

"Ladies and gentlemen, the government has wasted all of our time trying to convict a man for crimes they've already arrested the perpetrators for. They made up this conspiracy theory because of associations. My client grew up with some of the witnesses, is that a crime? No. He employed or went into legitimate business with some of them, there's definitely no crime in that but just because some of his friends are criminals that doesn't mean he did the crimes they did. It means he chose the wrong friends. And I'll tell you this, he didn't get indicted on a charge called choosing the wrong friends in the first degree. After viewing the evidence, I urge you, ladies and gentleman, to do what the law tells you when the government hasn't reached its burden. You acquit. Thank you."

Afterthought

Nafiys

Ms. Weinstein is a beast.   She played her part in that courtroom. I can't front for a minute I thought it was a wrap.   But when Trish flipped the script, things changed then to put the icing on the cake Class goes missing. Allah is definitely on my side. I don't know why Trish did what she did but I applaud her for that.   Maybe Bish's spirit moved in her and motivated her to do that. Or she probably thought of how he would've felt if he were alive. She loved that man and probably never loved any other. Her respect and adoration for him reached her from the grave.

As for Class maybe he couldn't do it no more. He probably couldn't live with himself, who knows? Whatever the case may be, he's still a rat. That don't go away. As for me, I'm in the Federal Detention Center waiting on the Jury's verdict. I still haven't spoken to Ryan. I hope she doesn't keep my son away from me; that wouldn't be right or fair. Last I heard, she is living with her friend Kwanda in Harlem. She won't be hard to find if that's the case. Then the lawyer continued to hammer at the government's case.

I got word that Corey is up in Leaven Worth. He did that interview for that magazine too. He's an idiot and a snake. Finding out that he did that interview, I sent a few kites through the prison system. One day Corey went to the yard to lift weights. He laid on a bench to bench-press and his face was introduced to a fifty pound dumb bell. His nose, cheek bone and jaw were smashed. They say when he healed he looked like he had an operation.

Chris, I heard is in Protective Custody in some federal camp somewhere in Pennsylvania. Beef is also in

P.C in a federal Prison in Terra Haute, Indiana serving 15 years. I heard Corey and Class' nephew, Malik, got indicted by the feds in New York on RICO charges. He'll be with his uncle Corey soon. I heard he refused an interview with that magazine. That's Thorough.

Little Butchie got 10 years. I hear he's in Fairton. A federal joint in Jersey. I know some dudes over there. He won't last long. If he gets kicked out of there or transferred, he'll run into my co-defendants on the armored truck robbery case I served 10 years for. My old head Bright is in Marion now. They all know little Butchie. He can't hide.

They gave Trish 12 years for the Conspiracy charge and sent her to a woman's prison in upstate New York; Lavelle makes sure she stays in contact with Coco. He sent her upstate with a friend to see Trish. Sadly Class' mom passed away. Form what I heard about her and how she was against Class' actions, the lady was a thoroughbred.

As for me, well I'm done with the game. I'm done dealing with a bunch of dudes who aren't loyal. I'm done thinking for cats who should be able to think for themselves and as far as meeting new friends.

"Hey, yo name Nafiys?" this young cat asked me as I shot a few balls on the court in the prison's gym.

"Yeah, why, what's it to you?" I asked ready to attack this dude. I saw the fear on his face as I dropped the ball as if I was ready to lunge at him.

"I don't want no problems, man. I just wanted to meet you. I'm from West Park, I heard a lot about you. I'm about getting money. Maybe one day when you get out................."

I cut him off immediately. "Listen homey, I'm cool I'm not tryna get to know you, you dig."

"Yeah I can dig it," the young cat said as I walked out of the gym. I went to my cell, read the Quran until I was tired. I made my last prayer for the day. I prayed that I would come out of this a free man. I prayed that I could raise my son the right way; in the way of Prophet Muhammad. I prayed for a lot of young and old black men warehoused in these concentration camps. Hopefully a lot of them will emerge from these mental graves and warehouses as responsible men. Prepared to reverse the damage they've helped to create in their communities. I prayed for my own sense of righteousness and consciousness. I have to be a Muslim to the fullest extent and stop thinking I can continue to have one foot in the hell fire and one foot out. I must stop being selfish in my thoughts and think of who else I'm hurting and is affected by my lifestyle. Family

All these prayers and thoughts ran through my mind until I fell asleep. The following morning I'm in a courtroom so quiet in anticipation to hear the words that would seal my fate from the 12 people who held it in their hands. I took one more look around the courtroom to see if Ryan was there. The spot were she usually sat was now occupied by a young white guy who looked like a journalist writing in a small notepad.

"Has the Jury reached a verdict? The deep voiced Judge asked looking over his glasses at the Jury

A tall heavy set baldhead white guy stood up in the jury box.

"Yes your honor, we have."

"Please hand the verdict slip to the bailiff," the judge ordered. The place was so quiet I could hear my heart beat. Life seems like it moves in slow motion in situations like this. The judge read the verdict slip to himself then nodded his head. I couldn't read the expression on his face after he read it. He showed no emotion or reaction to what he read.

But I don't think he or anyone in the courtroom was surprised when the foreman announced:

"We the jury, find the defendant, Nafiys Muhammad, not guilty!"

The New Beginning...

Sample Chapter

Hoodfellas II
American Gangster

Chapter 1

Haiti's clear skies, warm sunshine and inviting winds offer the perfect accommodating situation to explore the country's natural splendor. It's undiscovered, pristine trails, and foothills present the best opportunity for a serene bike ride. An abundance of outdoor opportunities reside in the back mountains of this precious island. The effervescent mood of the people is welcoming and embracing. With plenty of open spaces and green pasture for miles to come, warm climate and plenty of fresh Caribbean air, it's inexcusable to spend too much time indoor on this wonderful island. All of this aura brought a new sense of being to Deon Campbell. He felt rejuvenated when he first arrived in Haiti.

Deon thought he had left his criminal and troubled past behind and was hoping to start anew in a place where nobody knew his name. The fresh Caribbean air hit his face the minute he stepped off the cruise ship, and he just knew that the lifestyle of the rich and infamous was calling his name. With enough money to buy part of the island, Deon wouldn't have any financial worries until his calling from God. On the drive to Jean Paul's mansion caravan-style with a Toyota Sequoia ahead of him with armed security men and another Land Cruiser jeep filled with additional armed security men behind the limousine, Deon's mind was free to think about how he would miss his best friends and buddies, Short Dawg and No neck while riding in the air conditioned, long stretch limousine with his new friend, Jean Paul, and his entourage. He wanted to exact revenge on Short Dawg and No Neck's murderers and he would spend as much money it would take to make sure their killers don't live to see another day.

"I see you're a serious man and you're serious about your business," Deon said to Jean Paul as he sipped on a bottle of water while Jean Paul sipped on cognac. "In this country, you have to be. Don't let all the armed security intimidate you, it's a way of life here in Haiti," Jean Paul told him. An additional limousine also followed with all the luggage and money that Deon had to carry to Haiti with him. One of Deon's men rode with the second limousine driver. Keeping his eyes on the prize was very important and Deon didn't hide the fact that he wanted to know where his money was at all times. "I can't help but notice the worried look on your face, your money is fine. I have some of the best security men that Haiti has to offer…" and before the words could escape Jean Paul's mouth, gunfire erupted and bullets were flying everywhere from both sides of the road. A group of men emerged with machine guns as they attempted to stop the caravan so they could rob the crew. Deon had been in battle before, but this shit was ten times more than he had ever seen and he didn't know if Jean Paul had set him up or if they were just being robbed. "This fucking Haitian posse bullshit again!" Jean Paul screamed out loud. "Don't worry about a thing. All the cars are bullet proof down to the tires, but we're gonna teach these bastards a lesson, so they'll never fuck with me again. In each of those little compartments next to the button to lock your door is a nickel plated 9 millimeter, you guys are free to take out as many of them as possible. Their lives are worth shit here," he told them. At the push of a button, Jean Paul opened his compartment and pulled out two loaded .45 Lugar's. He cracked opened his window, and aimed at the pedestrian robbers. The crew of almost 20 men stood no chance as Jean Paul and his men returned fire with high powered guns from the barricaded bullet proof windows of the vehicles. A raid in Vietnam wouldn't even compare to the massacre that went on for about 2 minutes. After all the men were down, Jean Paul got out of the car to make sure that none of them had any breath left in them. It was like a firing squad as his men went around unloading bullets in the bodies lying across the pavement, ensuring that every one of the robbers was dead! The last crawling survivor received two bullets in each knee and one to the head before revealing that he was part of the Haitian posse located in the slums of Cite Soleil, the most dangerous slum in Port-Au-Prince, Haiti.

Even the United Nations guards, who are sent to monitor the situation in Haiti, were too afraid to go into Cite Soleil. The Haitian police feared confrontation in the slums because they were always outgunned and very few officers who went against the gang lived to tell about it another day. Jean Paul had been a target ever since his arrival in Haiti because he never hid his lavish lifestyle. A brash former drug dealer who grew up in the States, and was deported back to his homeland some twenty years later, he was not accustomed to the Haitian lifestyle or Haitian culture. After arriving in Haiti, Jean Paul had to learn his culture all over again. Americans like to say they're hungry enough to go do something drastic to feed their family, but in Haiti, those people literally lived it. Forced to eat dirt cookies due to lack of food, money and other resources, these gang members were tired of being hungry and anybody who got in their paths will pay the price for a better life, or better yet, food.

Many Haitian immigrants left Haiti with the hopes to one day go back to their homeland to help with the financial, economical, social infrastructure as well as democratic leadership. However, many of them usually find that what they left behind some twenty to thirty years ago has changed to the worst Haiti that they have ever seen. Since the departure of Baby Doc, Haiti has taken a turn for the worst and the economic climate in Haiti has forced many of its delinquents to become criminals of the worst kinds. While in the United States poor families are offered food stamps, subsidized housing and other economic relief by the government; in Haiti, relief only comes in the form of money sent to those who have relatives who live abroad. Those without relatives abroad suffer the worst kind of inhumane treatment, hunger, malnourishment, social inadequacies and the worst health.

To top off an already problematic situation, many of the Haitian politicians are unconscionable thieves who look to fill their pockets while the country is in dire need of every imaginable resource possible, including, but not limited to jobs, healthcare, social programs, education, clean water, deforestation, land development, any kind of industry and so on. Many of the elected officials offer promises, but rarely deliver on the promises after taking office. Most of the time, they become puppets of the United States government and in turn, look for their own self-interest instead of the interest of the people. Deon had no idea what he was stepping into and on the surface it appeared as if he would lead a peaceful life in the first Black republic of the world.

There's a price to be paid for freedom and winning a war against Napoleon's super French army with machetes and pure heart of warriors, the Haitians are definitely paying a price for it now. A brief history on the country was given to Deon and his crew by Jean Paul while on their three-hour drive to Jacmel from Port-Au-Prince where Jean Paul resided. Deon learned how Haiti, known back then as the pearl of the Antilles, has lost its luster and every resource it used to own due to deforestation. Coffee, sugarcane, cocoa and mangos are just a few of the natural resources and national products that the country used to offer the world, but most of it has evaporated because the government has not provided any assistance to the people to help them become self-sufficient in farming and land development. Security is one of the major reasons why foreign companies stay out of Haiti, and the government is not doing anything to bring back those companies as well as tourism, which helped the country thrive under the leadership of dirty old Papa Doc.

It was disheartening to Deon and his crew as they watched little kids running wild on the street digging through piles of trash looking for food along with the wild pigs and dogs on the side of the roads. Their faces reeked of pain, loneliness, hunger, starvation, malnutrition and hopelessness. Most of Deon's roughneck crew members were teary eyed as they watched this for almost two hours during the drive before hitting the scenic part of Haiti. Undeterred by the events that took place in the capital a few hours earlier, Deon ordered the driver to pull over in the center of St. Marc to hand out hundred dollar bills to a group of hungry children. The whole crew took part in handing out the money to the children who looked like they hadn't eaten a good meal since birth. Cindy took it especially hard as she was the only woman amongst the crew and Jean Paul didn't hide the fact that the minority two percent of white people in Haiti and another ten percent of mullatoes and people of mixed heritage controlled the wealth of Haiti.

It was evident who the wealthy people in Haiti were as they drove around in their frosty Range Rovers, Land Cruisers and other big name SUV's with their windows up as they navigate through the ghetto to rape the people of their wealth during the day while they rest their heads in their mansion in the Hills at night. The children rejoiced as Deon and the crew gave them enough money that would probably last them a whole month and more, to feed themselves and their families. Jean Paul was happy to see that his new friends sympathized with the people of Haiti, but he cautioned for them not to allow their kindness to become a habit as it could be detrimental to their livelihood.

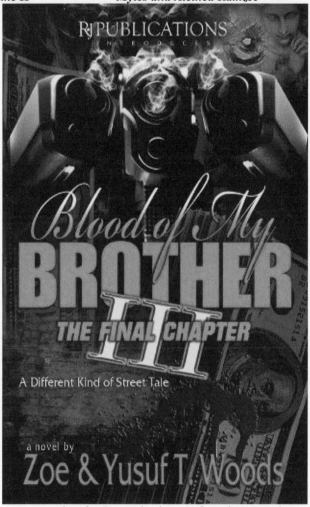

Retiring is no longer an option for Roc, who is now forced to restudy Philly's vicious streets through blood filled eyes. He realizes that his brother's killer is none other than his mentor, Mr. Holmes. With this knowledge, the strategic game of chess that began with the pushing of a pawn in the Blood of My Brother series, symbolizes one of love, loyalty, blood, mayhem, and death. In the end, the streets of Philadelphia will never be the same...

In Storess!!!

After Chasin' Satisfaction, Julius finds that satisfaction is not all that it's cracked up to be. It left nothing but death in its aftermath. Now living the glamorous life in Miami while putting the finishing touches on his hybrid condo hotel, he realizes with newfound success he's now become the hunted. Julian's success is threatened as someone from his past vows revenge on him.

In Stores!!!

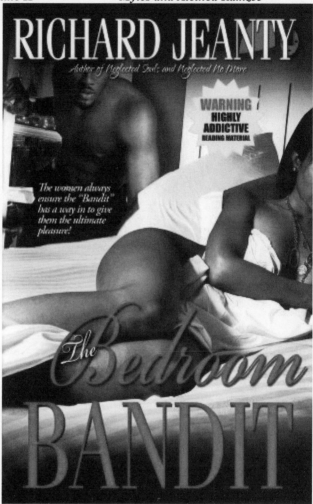

It may not be Histeria Lane, but these desperate housewives are fed up with their neglecting husbands. Their sexual needs take precedence over the millions of dollars their husbands bring home every year to keep them happy in their affluent neighborhood. While their husbands claim to be hard at work, these wives are doing a little work of their own with the bedroom bandit. Is the bandit swift enough to evade these angry husbands?

In Stores!!

NEGLECTED SOULS

Motherhood and the trials of loving too hard and not enough frame this story...The realism of these characters will bring tears to your spirit as you discover the hero in the villain you never saw coming...

In Stores!!!

Jimmy and Nina continue to feel a void in their lives because they haven't a clue about their genealogical make-up. Jimmy falls victims to a life threatening illness and only the right organ donor can save his life. Will the donor be the bridge to reconnect Jimmy and Nina to their biological family? Will Nina be the strength for her brother in his time of need? Will they ever find out what really happened to their mother?

In Stores!!!

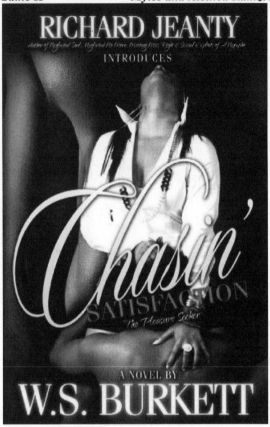

Betrayal, lust, lies, murder, deception, sex and tainted love frame this story... Julian Stevens lacks the ambition and freak ability that Miko looks for in a man, but she married him despite his flaws to spite an ex-boyfriend. When Miko least expects it, the old boyfriend shows up and ready to sweep her off her feet again. She wants to have her cake and eat it too. While Miko's doing her own thing, Julian is determined to become everything Miko ever wanted in a man and more, but will he go to extreme lengths to prove he's worthy of Miko's love? Julian Stevens soon finds out that he's capable of being more than he could ever imagine as he embarks on a journey that will change his life forever.

In Stores!!!

The police in New York and other major cities around the country are increasingly victimizing black men. The violence has escalated to deadly force, most of the time without justification. In this controversial book, noted author Richard Jeanty, tackles the problem of police brutality and the unfair treatment of Black men at the hands of police in New York City and the rest of the country.

In Stores!!!

Just when Darren thinks his relationship with Tina is flourishing, there is yet another hurdle on the road hindering their bliss. Tina saw a therapist for months to deal with her sexual addiction, but now Darren is wondering if she was ever treated completely. Darren has not been taking care of home and Tina's frustrated and agrees to a break-up with Darren. Will Darren lose Tina for good? Will Tina ever realize that Darren is the best man for her?

In Stores!!

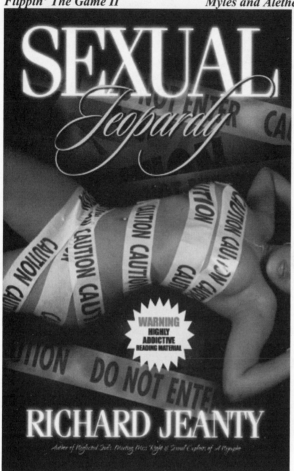

Ronald Murphy was a player all his life until he and his best friend, Myles, met the women of their dreams during a brief vacation in South Beach, Florida. Sexual Jeopardy is story of trust, betrayal, forgiveness, friendship and hope.

In Stores!!!

Tina develops an insatiable sexual appetite very early in life. She
only loves her boyfriend, Darren, but he's too far away in college to satisfy her sexual needs.
Tina decides to get buck wild away in college
Will her sexual trysts jeopardize the lives of the men in her life?

In Stores!!!

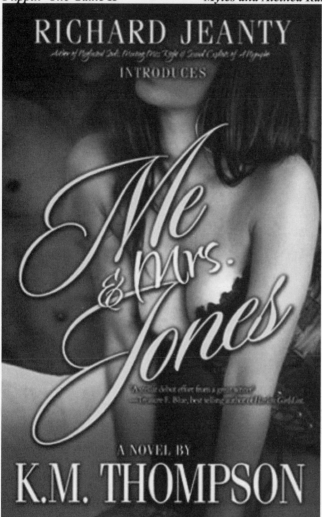

Faith Jones, a woman in her mid-thirties, has given up on ever finding love again until she met her son's best friend, Darius. Faith Jones is walking a thin line of betrayal against her son for the love of Darius. Will Faith allow her emotions to outweigh her common sense?

In Stores!!!

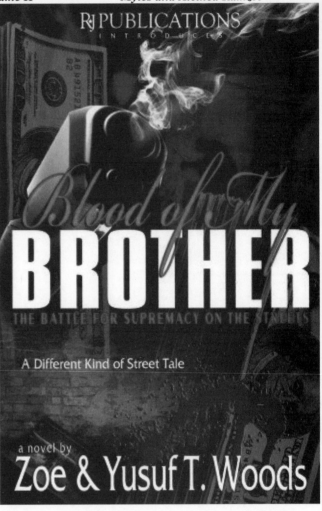

Roc was the man on the streets of Philadelphia, until his younger brother decided it was time to become his own man by wreaking havoc on Roc's crew without any regards for the blood relation they share. Drug, murder, mayhem and the pursuit of happiness can lead to deadly consequences. This story can only be told by a person who has lived it.

In Stores!!!

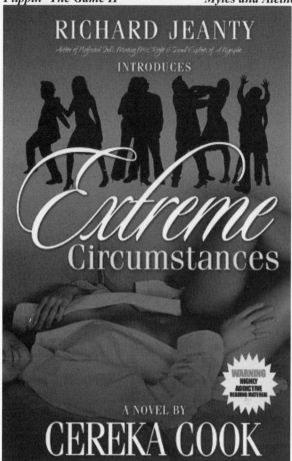

What happens when a devoted woman is betrayed? Come take a ride with Chanel as she takes her boyfriend, Donnell, to circumstances beyond belief after he betrays her trust with his endless infidelities. How long can Chanel's friend, Janai, use her looks to get what she wants from men before it catches up to her? Find out as Janai's gold-digging ways catch up with and she has to face the consequences of her extreme actions.

In Stores!!!

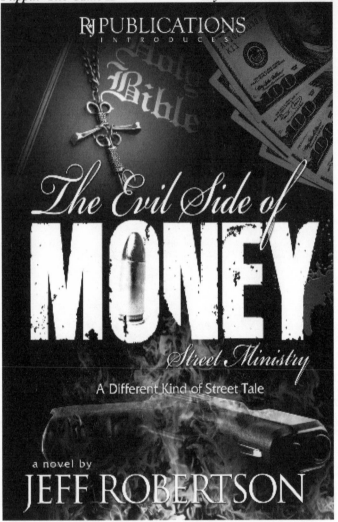

Violence, Intimidation and carnage are the order as Nathan and his brother set out to build the most powerful drug empires in Chicago. However, when God comes knocking, Nathan's conscience starts to surface. Will his haunted criminal past get the best of him?

In Stores!!

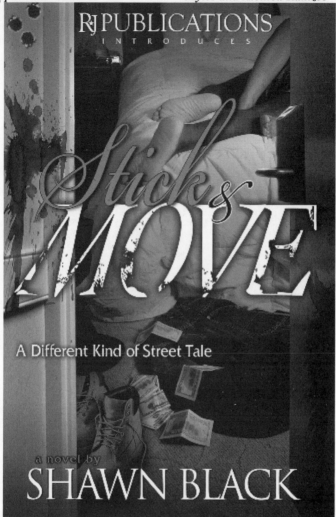

RJ PUBLICATIONS
I N T R O D U C E S

Stick & MOVE

A Different Kind of Street Tale

a novel by
SHAWN BLACK

Yasmina witnessed the brutal murder of her parents at a young age at the hand of a drug dealer. This event stained her mind and upbringing as a result. Will Yamina's life come full circle with her past? Find out as Yasmina's crew, The Platinum Chicks, set out to make a name for themselves on the street.

In stores!!

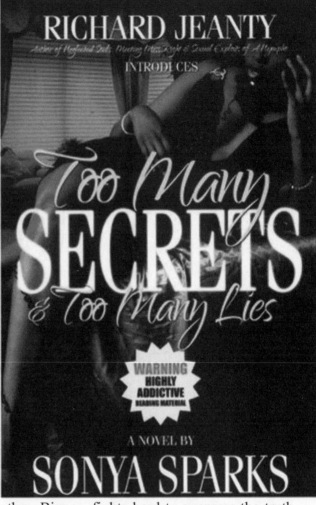

Ashland's mother, Bianca, fights hard to suppress the truth from her daughter because she doesn't want her to marry Jordan, the grandson of an ex-lover she loathes. Ashland soon finds out how cruel and vengeful her mother can be, but what price will Bianca pay for redemption?

In stores!!

Malcolm is a wealthy virgin who decides to conceal his wealth
From the world until he meets the right woman. His wealthy best
friend, Dexter, hides his wealth from no one. Malcolm struggles to
find love in an environment where vanity and materialism are
rampant, while Dexter is getting more than enough of his share of
women. Malcolm needs develop self-esteem and confidence to
meet the right woman and Dexter's confidence is borderline
arrogance.
Will bad boys like Dexter continue to take women for a ride?

Or will nice guys like Malcolm continue to finish last?

In Stores!!!

RICHARD JEANTY

INTRODUCES

WARNING
HIGHLY
ADDICTIVE

Cater to Her

A NOVEL BY
SEAN MITCHELL

What happens when a woman's devotion to her fiancee is tested weeks before she gets married? What if her fiancee is just hiding behind the veil of ministry to deceive her? Find out as Sean Mitchell takes you on a journey you'll never forget into the lives of Angelica, Titus and Aurelius.

In Stores!!

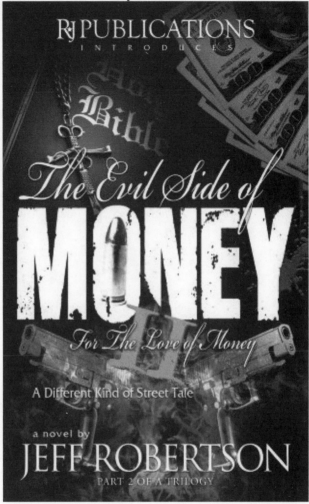

A beautigul woman from Bolivia threatens the existence of the drug empire that Nate and G have built. While Nate is head over heels for her, G can see right through her. As she brings on more conflict between the crew, G sets out to show Nate exactly who she is before she brings about their demise.

In Stores!!!

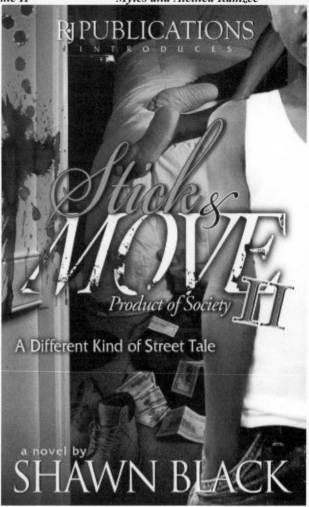

Scorcher and Yasmina's low key lifestyle was interrupted when they were taken down by the Feds, but their daughter, Serosa, was left to be raised by the foster care system. Will Serosa become a product of her environment or will she rise above it all? Her bloodline is undeniable, but will she be able to control it?

In Stores!!

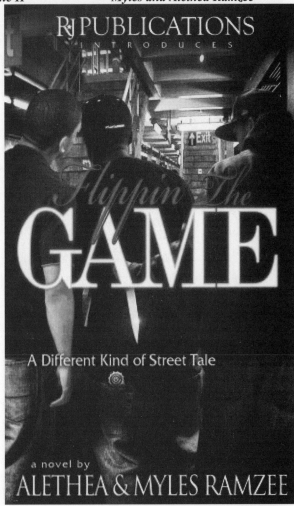

An ex-drug dealer finds himself in a bind after he's caught by the Feds. He has to decide which is more important, his family or his loyalty to the game. As he fights hard to make a decision, those who helped him to the top fear the worse from him. Will he get the chance to tell the govt. whole story, or will someone get to him before he becomes a snitch?

In Stores!!!

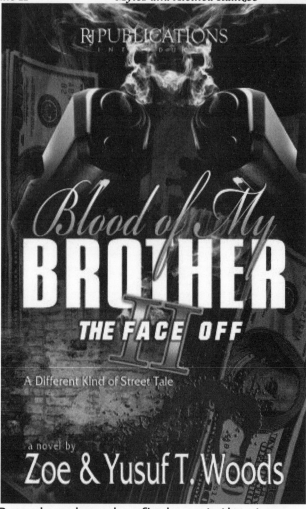

What will Roc do when he finds out the true identity of Solo? Will the blood shed come from his own brother Lil Mac? Will Roc and Solo take their beef to an explosive height on the street? Find out as Zoe and Yusuf bring the second installment to their hot street joint, Blood of My Brother.

In Stores!!!

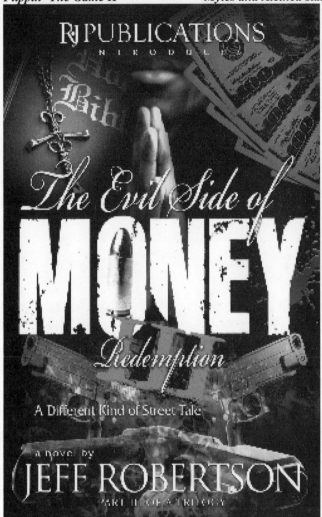

Forced to abandon the drug world for good, Nathan and G attempt to change their lives and move forward, but will their past come back to haunt them? This final installment will leave you speechless.

In Stores!!!

Dave Richardson is enjoying success as his second book became a New York Times best-seller. He left the life of The Bedroom behind to settle with his family, but an obsessed fan has not had enough of Dave and she will go to great length to get a piece of him. How far will a woman go to get a man that doesn't belong to her?

Coming September 2010

Deon is at the mercy of a ruthless gang that kidnapped him. In a foreign land where he knows nothing about the culture, he has to use his survival instincts and his wit to outsmart his captors. Will the Hoodfellas show up in time to rescue Deon, or will Crazy D take over once again and fight an all out war by himself?

Coming March 2010

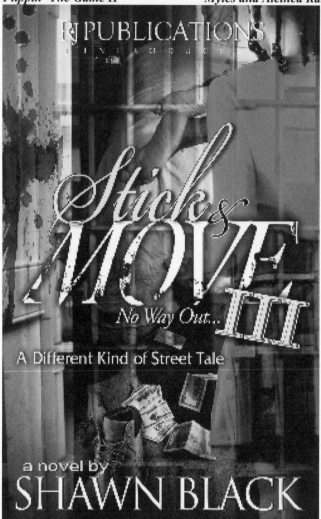

While Yasmina sits on death row awaiting her fate, her daughter, Serosa, is fighting the fight of her life on the outside. Her genetic structure that indirectly bins her to her parents could also be her downfall and force her to see that there's no way out!

Coming January 2010

The drama continues as Deshun is hunted by Angela who still feels that ex-girlfriend Kayla is still trying to win his heart, though he brutally raped her. Angela will kill anyone who gets in her way, but is DeShun worth all the aggravation?

In Stores!!!

Buck Johnson was forced to make the best out of worst situation. He has witnessed the most cruel events in his life and it is those events who the man that he has become. Was the Johnson family ignorant souls through no fault of their own?

In Stores!!!

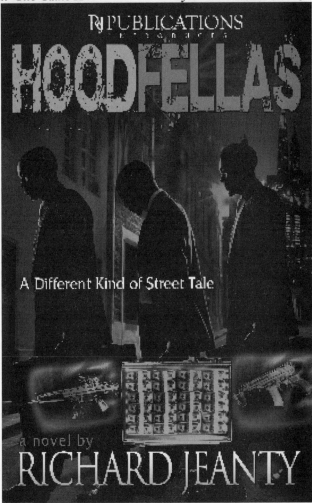

When an Ex-con finds himself destitute and in dire need of the basic necessities after he's released from prison, he turns to what he knows best, crime, but at what cost? Extortion, murder and mayhem drives him back to the top, but will he stay there?

In Stores !!!

What happens when someone falls insanely in love?
Stalking is just the beginning.
In Stores!!!

Use this coupon to order by mail

1.   Neglected Souls, Richard Jeanty $14.95
2.   Neglected No More, Richard Jeanty $14.95
3.   Ignorant Souls, Richard Jeanty $15.00, October 2009
4.   Sexual Exploits of Nympho, Richard Jeanty $14.95
5.   Meeting Ms. Right's Whip Appeal, Richard Jeanty $14.95
6.   Me and Mrs. Jones, K.M Thompson $14.95
7.   Chasin' Satisfaction, W.S Burkett $14.95
8.   Extreme Circumstances, Cereka Cook $14.95
9.   The Most Dangerous Gang In America, R. Jeanty $15.00
10. Sexual Exploits of a Nympho II, Richard Jeanty $15.00
11. Sexual Jeopardy, Richard Jeanty $14.95
12. Too Many Secrets, Too Many Lies, Sonya Sparks $15.00
13. Stick And Move, Shawn Black $15.00 Available
14. Evil Side Of Money, Jeff Robertson $15.00
15. Evil Side Of Money II, Jeff Robertson $15.00
16. Evil Side Of Money III, Jeff Robertson $15.00
17. Flippin' The Game, Alethea and M. Ramzee, $15.00 Available
18. Flippin' The Game II, Alethea and M. Ramzee, $15.00 Dec. 2009
19. Cater To Her, W.S Burkett $15.00
20. Blood of My Brother I, Zoe & Yusuf Woods $15.00
21. Blood of my Brother II, Zoe & Ysuf Woods $15.00
22. Hoodfellas, Richard Jeanty $15.00 available
23. Hoodfellas II, Richard Jeanty, $15.00 03/30/2010
24. The Bedroom Bandit, Richard Jeanty $15.00 Available
25. Mr. Erotica, Richard Jeanty, $15.00, Sept 2010
26. Stick N Move II, Shawn Black $15.00 Available
27. Stick N Move III, Shawn Black $15.00 Jan, 2010
28. Miami Noire, W.S. Burkett $15.00 Available
29. Insanely In Love, Cereka Cook $15.00 Available
30. Blood of My Brother III, Zoe & Yusuf Woods September 2009

Name_____

Address_____

City_____State_____Zip Code_____

Please send the novels that I have circled above.

Shipping and Handling: Free

Total Number of Books_____

Total Amount Due_____

Buy 3 books and get 1 free. This offer is subject to change without notice.

Send institution check or money order (no cash or CODs) to:

RJ Publications

PO Box 300771

Jamaica, NY 11434

For more information please call 718-471-2926, or visit www.rjpublications.com

Please allow 2-3 weeks for delivery.

Use this coupon to order by mail

31. Neglected Souls, Richard Jeanty $14.95
32. Neglected No More, Richard Jeanty $14.95
33. Ignorant Souls, Richard Jeanty $15.00, October 2009
34. Sexual Exploits of Nympho, Richard Jeanty $14.95
35. Meeting Ms. Right's Whip Appeal, Richard Jeanty $14.95
36. Me and Mrs. Jones, K.M Thompson $14.95
37. Chasin' Satisfaction, W.S Burkett $14.95
38. Extreme Circumstances, Cereka Cook $14.95
39. The Most Dangerous Gang In America, R. Jeanty $15.00
40. Sexual Exploits of a Nympho II, Richard Jeanty $15.00
41. Sexual Jeopardy, Richard Jeanty $14.95
42. Too Many Secrets, Too Many Lies, Sonya Sparks $15.00
43. Stick And Move, Shawn Black $15.00 Available
44. Evil Side Of Money, Jeff Robertson $15.00
45. Evil Side Of Money II, Jeff Robertson $15.00
46. Evil Side Of Money III, Jeff Robertson $15.00
47. Flippin' The Game, Alethea and M. Ramzee, $15.00 Available
48. Flippin' The Game II, Alethea and M. Ramzee, $15.00 Dec. 2009
49. Cater To Her, W.S Burkett $15.00
50. Blood of My Brother I, Zoe & Yusuf Woods $15.00
51. Blood of my Brother II, Zoe & Ysuf Woods $15.00
52. Hoodfellas, Richard Jeanty $15.00 available
53. Hoodfellas II, Richard Jeanty, $15.00 03/30/2010
54. The Bedroom Bandit, Richard Jeanty $15.00 Available
55. Mr. Erotica, Richard Jeanty, $15.00, Sept 2010
56. Stick N Move II, Shawn Black $15.00 Available
57. Stick N Move III, Shawn Black $15.00 Jan, 2010
58. Miami Noire, W.S. Burkett $15.00 Available
59. Insanely In Love, Cereka Cook $15.00 Available
60. Blood of My Brother III, Zoe & Yusuf Woods September 2009

Name_____

Address_____

City_____State_____Zip Code_____

Please send the novels that I have circled above.

Shipping and Handling: Free

Total Number of Books_____

Total Amount Due_____

Buy 3 books and get 1 free. This offer is subject to change without notice.
Send institution check or money order (no cash or CODs) to:

RJ Publications

PO Box 300771

Jamaica, NY 11434

For more information please call 718-471-2926, or visit www.rjpublications.com

Please allow 2-3 weeks for delivery.